Hunky Parker is watching you

Hunky Parker
is watching you

Gillian Cross

Illustrated by
Maureen Bradley

Oxford University Press

Oxford University Press, Walton Street, Oxford OX2 6DP

Oxford   New York   Toronto
Delhi   Bombay   Calcutta   Madras   Karachi
Kuala Lumpur   Singapore   Hong Kong   Tokyo
Nairobi   Dar es Salaam   Cape Town
Melbourne   Auckland   Madrid

and associated companies in
Berlin   Ibadan

Oxford is a trade mark of Oxford University Press

Copyright © Gillian Cross 1994
First published 1994

A CIP catalogue record for this book is available
from the British Library

ISBN 0 19 271705 7

Printed in Great Britain

Contents

Chapter 1

Ingrid is Back!

'Dinah!' Lloyd raced up the stairs and hammered on her bedroom door. 'Are you in there? Ingrid's back!'

There was no answer.

He thumped the door again. 'Ingrid's back! We're going to have a welcome home party in the SPLAT shed. Now. Are you coming?'

Still no answer.

'Purple pickled onions!' Impatiently, Lloyd pushed the door open and burst into the room.

Dinah was curled up on her bed, reading. Lloyd marched across and glanced at the book.

'What have you got there? *Further Advanced Mathematics*? Yuck! Why do you always read such weird things?'

'Mmm?' Dinah looked up and blinked. 'Oh, it's you. What's up?'

'I'm not telling you again,' Lloyd said, crossly. 'Stay there and read your boring old book if you want to. Harvey and I are off to the SPLAT shed.'

'Hang on a minute and I'll come too.' Dinah slipped the book into her pocket and stood up. 'Why are you in such a rush? Is something special happening?'

Lloyd spluttered and rolled his eyes up to the ceiling. 'You'll have to wait and see.'

Then Harvey rattled up the stairs, puffing and panting. 'Aren't you two ready *yet*? Ingrid'll be there first if we don't hurry.'

'Ingrid?' Dinah beamed. 'Is she back? I thought she was still in Wales.'

Lloyd gritted his teeth. 'Listen, Dinah. *Ingrid . . . Is . . . Back*. Got that? The spots have gone, and she's better, and she's come home. And we're going to do a Grand Welcome in the SPLAT shed. *If* we get there in time.'

'Why didn't you say so?'

Dinah leapt down the stairs, grabbed her coat and raced through the front door. Lloyd pulled a face.

'Just think — we *asked* Mum and Dad to adopt her. We must have been mad. Life was much simpler before she came.'

'When the Headmaster was here?' Harvey gaped. 'You *liked* it when everyone else was hypnotized?'

'Of course not,' said Lloyd. 'I just meant —'

But Harvey had stopped listening. He was marching down the stairs like a robot, chanting in a mechanical voice, 'You Will Do What I Say. The Headmaster Is A Marvellous Man, And This Is The Best School I've Ever Been To.'

He ran off after Dinah and Lloyd followed, shaking his head. Everyone in SPLAT was getting *impossible*. It had been dreadful when the Headmaster was there, but at least they'd had something to struggle against. When there were only five of them who couldn't be hypnotized. But now . . .

2

Lloyd trudged down an alley and through the gate at the bottom. By the time he reached the SPLAT shed, Dinah and Harvey were already there, knocking on the door.

Mandy's voice came from inside. 'The man who can keep order can rule the world.'

Lloyd finished the password. 'But the man who can bear disorder is truly free.'

Then he pushed open the door. Mandy was spreading a cloth over the box they used for a table and she looked up and smiled.

'Did you get my message? You know Ingrid's back?'

'Oh yes,' said Lloyd. 'We all know. Even Dinah.' He pulled a face at her. 'What about Ian?'

'He's gone to get some lemonade,' Mandy said. 'There's lots of money in the SPLAT savings, and I thought — oh, here he is.'

Ian lounged in, not bothering with the password, and put three bottles of lemonade on the table.

He grinned at Lloyd. 'Have you heard? Ingrid's back!'

'Shimmering scarlet sausages!' Lloyd thought he was going to explode. 'Of course I've heard! But why are we all *talking* about it. We've got to get this welcome *organized* — or she'll be here. What are we going to do?'

'I've made a cake,' Mandy said.

She lifted it out of her bag and put it on the table. It was a big cake with white icing and pink letters all over it. The big ones across the top said *Welcome Home Ingrid* and the little ones round the sides spelt out SPLAT's full

3

name: *Society for the Protection of our Lives Against Them.*

'I thought we could sing a song before we cut it,' Mandy said.

'Really?' Ian raised his eyebrows. 'How about "Happy Birthday"?'

'Ha ha,' said Lloyd.

But Harvey was bounding up and down. 'That'll do! It will! We can change the words to "Welcome Back Home to You". Like this.

Welcome back home to you!
Welcome back home to you!
Welcome back home, dear Ingrid . . .'

Lloyd put his hands over his ears. 'We'll have to practise —'

But they'd run out of time. The gate creaked and there was a knock on the shed door.

'Hallo?' said a voice from outside. 'Anyone there?'

Lloyd put his finger to his lips and lifted his hand. 'We'll sing what Harvey said,' he hissed. 'Start when I drop my hand.' He raised his voice and called out the first half of the password. 'The man who can keep order can rule the world.'

'Oh, you don't need to bother with *that*,' Ingrid said impatiently. 'It's only me.'

She pushed at the door.

'Get ready!' whispered Lloyd, still with his hand in the air.

The door swung open and Ingrid bounced into the

4

shed. Spreading her arms wide, she grinned at them and whirled round.

'I'm back!'

Lloyd brought his hand down.

But no one sang a word. They were too startled. All of them were staring in amazement at what Ingrid was wearing.

Ian was the first to get his breath back. 'That's a pretty nasty T-shirt,' he drawled.

Ingrid beamed. 'Isn't it *disgusting*?' She whirled round again, more slowly this time, making sure they didn't miss anything.

On the front of the T-shirt was a close-up of a pig's face, with a disgusting, slobbery snout. The face was grinning triumphantly and large black letters were printed underneath it.

WHO'S ALWAYS RIGHT?

On the back was another version of the same face. This time, there was pig-swill dribbling from its mouth and the words underneath were different.

I'm an ED-u-cated pig!

Harvey shuddered. 'How can you bear to wear it?'

'I was afraid you'd all have them too,' Ingrid said happily. 'But I can see I'm the first. *Who's always right?*'

She whirled again, and then slowed down as she took in their expressions.

'You mean it, don't you?' she said, in an astonished voice. 'You really *don't* like it.'

'I'm sorry,' Mandy said apologetically, 'but it makes me feel sick. I don't think I can eat any cake if I have to look at it. I've never seen anything like it.'

Ingrid's mouth dropped open. 'You mean — they're not all over the shops? But you can't buy anything else in Wales. Everything's Hunky Parker there.'

Ian raised his eyebrows. 'Everything's *what*?'

'Hunky Parker. Oh, come *on*. You must have heard of Hunky Parker. He's been on television for four weeks.'

'Not here he hasn't,' said Lloyd.

Ingrid stared at him. Then she glanced at the others. All their faces were blank and, for a second, she looked taken aback. Then she grinned.

'Well, he soon will be. He's just *brilliant*. If you come back to my house after the cake, I'll show you my video.'

'I don't think —' Mandy began.

But Lloyd didn't let her finish. He hated the T-shirt too, but he liked to know what was going on.

'We'll all come,' he said firmly. 'After the lemonade and the cake. We'll watch the video together.'

'SPLAT meets Hunky Parker!' Ingrid giggled. 'You wait. You'll just love it. I know you will. *I'm an ED-u-cated pig!*'

She grabbed the cake and cut it into six big slices. Then she sat back and bit into one of them.

It was six o'clock before they got to Ingrid's. Dinah tried to slip off home, but Lloyd wouldn't let her.

'This is a SPLAT meeting, and that means we stick together. You've *got* to come.'

Dinah didn't look pleased, but she went to Ingrid's and sat down in the front room, with the rest of them.

'It's not a very long video,' Ingrid said, as she pulled out the cassette. 'Only a quarter of an hour. But it's fantastic. This was the first Hunky Parker programme Aunty Rachel let me watch, and I was still quite ill then. But the moment I saw it I was hooked.'

7

She switched the video on and sat back, with a pleased expression on her face. Almost immediately, the screen was filled by a huge, slobbery pig's face, exactly the same as the one on the front of her T-shirt. It cocked its head and spoke smugly.

'*Who's always right?*'

A hundred voices roared the answer, as the words splashed across the screen.

'HUNKY PARKER!!!'

The pig blew a raspberry, drooling bubbles from its snout. Then it waddled away from the camera, into a neat, clean kitchen, where the table was laid for breakfast.

'I just love eating with the family,' it said. 'I'm an ED-u-cated pig!'

Seizing a packet of cornflakes, it began to tip them into its mouth, showering crumbs all over the table.

Lloyd stared. Ingrid thought *this* was brilliant? Had she gone mad? He didn't know if he could sit through a quarter of an hour of it.

He looked round at the others. Dinah had already given up. She'd slipped the maths book out of her pocket and was reading that, totally ignoring the video. Lloyd shook his head. He ought to *make* her watch. But how could he, when the video was such rubbish?

Glancing back at the screen, he saw Hunky Parker pick up a tin of golden syrup and empty it on to the table, on top of the sugar and toast and cornflakes he'd already spilt. *Bor-ing*, Lloyd thought.

And then something very odd happened.

While Hunky Parker was spilling the golden syrup, he just looked horrible. Fat and smug and grubby. But, as he threw the tin on to the floor, something changed.

Not Hunky Parker himself. He was just as fat and smug and grubby as before. The change was in Lloyd's mind. Suddenly, that fatness and smugness and grubbiness wasn't horrible any more. Hunky Parker looked at the camera, grinned a dribbling grin and said, '*Who's always right?*' — and Lloyd found himself laughing.

He would have felt silly, but Mandy and Ian and Harvey were laughing too. And Ingrid was clutching her sides and rolling around on the couch. Only Dinah was quiet, buried in her book. How *could* she? When Hunky Parker was so . . . so . . .

When the video finished, Lloyd was still hunting for the right word. Funny? Smart? Clever? Those were all wrong. He couldn't think of any way of describing how he felt about Hunky Parker. He was just — It. The thing there had to be more of.

Looking at Ingrid, Lloyd began to wonder where he could buy a T-shirt like hers. He was going to ask, but Mandy got in first.

'You know your Aunty Rachel, Ingrid? In Wales?'

Ingrid nodded.

'If I sent her some money, d'you think she'd buy me a Hunky Parker T-shirt?'

'And me!' said Harvey.

'I fancy one too,' murmured Ian.

9

So do I, Lloyd was going to say — when he had a much better idea. A fantastic idea. He beamed at Ingrid and waved a hand towards her T-shirt.

'We'll *all* have one. *They can be SPLAT uniform!*'

Ingrid clapped her hands and Harvey bounced up and down with delight.

'That's brilliant! Fantastic!'

Lloyd grinned triumphantly. He didn't notice that Dinah was still deep in her maths book.

She hadn't heard a word.

Chapter 2

Hunkymania

A fortnight later, Dinah was sitting at breakfast with Lloyd and Harvey, quietly writing a computer program while she ate her porridge. Suddenly, there was a knock on the back door and Ingrid burst in.

'They've come! The postman's just brought them! I couldn't wait until nine o'clock to show you!'

'The T-shirts?' Lloyd grabbed the bundle.

'It's *wonderful* timing!' Ingrid said. 'Because — guess what! Hunky Parker's going to be on television here. Starting tomorrow.'

'Brilliant!' Lloyd had already pulled on a T-shirt. He held out two more to Harvey and Dinah. 'Come on. Let's see what we all look like together.'

Harvey grabbed his, but Dinah was still thinking about computers and she looked up, blinking. 'What is it?'

'Your T-shirt.' Lloyd shook it impatiently. 'We've bought them with the SPLAT savings. To be our uniform.'

Dinah stared at the T-shirt. Hunky Parker's slimy snout was just under Lloyd's fingers. 'I don't want one.'

'Chocolate-coloured cabbages!' Lloyd slammed the T-shirt down on the table. 'If you'd only *listen . . .*!'

11

'You've got to have one,' Harvey said, tugging his on. 'Otherwise we won't all be the same.'

'But — ' Dinah looked at the fat, dirty pig's face on Harvey's chest. She wanted to be like the others. They were SPLAT, and they always stuck together. But — 'Do I have to?'

'Yes, you do,' Lloyd said. Their mother came in and he whirled round. 'Look, Mum! Isn't this fantastic!'

Mrs Hunter's mouth dropped open. 'Where on earth did you get those?'

'From my aunty in Wales,' Ingrid said, proudly. 'And they've come just in time, because — '

'Because Hunky Parker's on television tomorrow!' interrupted Harvey. 'We'll be the only people with T-shirts!'

Lloyd's eyes lit up. 'Let's wear them to school on Friday! All the others will be *sick* they haven't got them.'

'Wear them to school?' Mrs Hunter looked horrified.

'We're supposed to wear uniform,' muttered Dinah.

Lloyd pulled a rude face. 'You sound just like the old Headmaster. *All pupils here shall wear correct, green uniform.*'

Dinah glared, but Harvey and Ingrid were giggling and joining in.

'*Everything must be neat and tidy. Then we shall take over the world.*'

Mrs Hunter frowned. 'It's no good playing games. I'm not letting you out of the house in those T-shirts.'

Thank goodness! thought Dinah. She screwed hers into a

little, tight ball and pushed it into the pocket of her trousers.

But that was on Wednesday. On Thursday evening, things changed completely. Because Hunky Parker was on television.

When Dinah came downstairs after the programme, Mrs Hunter was chuckling.

'That pig's quite something, isn't he? I can't think why *you* didn't come and watch, Dinah.'

Lloyd's eyes gleamed. 'So what about our T-shirts?'

Mrs Hunter hesitated for a moment and then laughed. 'All right. You can wear them tomorrow if you like.'

'But — ' Dinah gulped. 'What about school uniform?'

'It won't matter for once,' said Mrs Hunter airily. She lifted up a clenched fist, grinning. 'HUN-KY PAR-KER — ALL RIGHT?'

Dinah folded her hands and looked down at the tablecloth, but no one noticed. Lloyd was busy planning their Grand Entrance into school the next morning.

'We march into the playground and stand in a line. OK? Then I shout "Hunky Parker!" — and we open our jackets!'

And show the T-shirts. Dinah could just imagine it. Six horrible pig-faces, slobbering in a row. Everyone would make sick noises, and she would have to stand there, pretending she liked Hunky Parker.

13

She shuddered, and pushed her plate away. It was going to be a nightmare.

But she was wrong. Completely wrong. The next morning, the six of them marched into the playground, just as Lloyd had planned, flung open their jackets, and . . . got mobbed. The moment they showed the T-shirts, everyone charged straight at them, yelling.

'You lucky — !'

'Where did you get those?'

'HUN-KY PAR-KER — YEAH!'

Lloyd beamed. He slipped his jacket off, to show the rest of the T-shirt, and bellowed above all the noise.

'They're very hard to get. But I know where!'

He was an instant hero.

Dinah could have sold her T-shirt ten times over that day — but she knew Lloyd would never forgive her if she did. Miserably she went on wearing it, longing for the end of school, so that she could forget all about Hunky Parker.

But when they walked out of the playground at home time, things got even worse.

'Look!' screeched Ingrid. She pointed across the road at the sweetshop. 'They've got Hunky too!'

The shabby little shop window was full of crisp packets and chocolate bars, with two banners draped across the top.

PIG OUT ON A HUNKY BAR!!
HUNKY CHUNKS ARE SWILLIANT!!!

The shop doorway was crowded with children fighting to get in, and other children coming out with their hands full of crisps and chocolate.

Harvey beamed. 'Oh *yes*!'

He and Ingrid charged across the road, right in front of a lorry, and Dinah gasped. 'Stop them, someone! Lloyd!'

But Lloyd was following. 'I'm getting across there before they scoff the lot. Those bars look brilliant.'

'*Swill*iant, you mean,' murmured Ian. 'Let's go!'

15

Even Mandy drifted over. In a few seconds, Dinah was standing alone on the pavement, staring at the struggling crowd in the shop doorway.

It's only a craze, she thought. *It'll go away.*

When Lloyd and Harvey came back across the road, they were sucking Hunky Bars and holding a packet of Hunky Chunks in their other hand.

'Want one?' Harvey held out his packet and chanted, 'Tasty Hunky Chunks, the ED-u-cated snack. Swill flavour.'

Dinah shuddered. 'Yuck! No thanks!'

'Please yourself.' Harvey took a bite of the chocolate bar and pushed a Hunky Chunk into his mouth as well. 'There aren't enough to go round, anyway. The shop was just about running out when we got there. I was really worried I might not get any.'

It's only a craze, Dinah thought again. But there was an unhappy, niggling feeling at the back of her mind.

Within a week, Hunky Parker was everywhere. All the children at school seemed to have Hunky socks, and Hunky watches, and Hunky pencil cases, and everything was *swilliant* or *ED-u-cated*.

The newspapers picked up the craze, too. They homed in on the bizarre way the programmes arrived at the television studio.

WHERE DOES HUNKY COME FROM???

said huge front page headlines on Thursday morning.

WILL HE MAKE IT??

Tonight, highly-paid TV executives will be crossing
their fingers and chewing their nails. At half-past six
— sharp! — thirty swillion viewers are expected to sit
down to watch The Pig.

And the programme won't reach the studio until
an hour before!!

On the dot of half-past five, a mystery woman on a
motor bike is supposed to roar into the Television
Centre, bringing the precious Hunky Parker tape
from a secret destination.

But suppose she doesn't make it?

Suppose something happens to her???

But nothing did happen to her. The programme went out
dead on half-past six. And Dinah felt like the only person
in the country not watching.

Next day, every shop on the way to school was
flaunting something with the slobbering pig's face
splashed across it. The baker's window was full of
Hunky Doughnuts (they're swilliant!) and there was
a huge, lurid poster plastered over the front of the
travel agency.

SUSS OUT THE STY!!
Holiday at Hunky's place for
SUN AND SNOW TOGETHER!!

Harvey pressed his nose to the window and sighed. 'If only we *could*! D'you think Mum and Dad would take us?'

'Never mind about that,' Lloyd said, impatiently. 'Look over there!'

He pointed at the shoe shop next to the school. There was a great heap of trainers in the window, and a huge poster of Hunky Parker's filthy face. Harvey started to run towards them.

'Come on!' he yelled over his shoulder. 'These are really ED-u-cated!'

Lloyd raced after him and Dinah trailed behind, wondering what could be so special about trainers.

She soon found out. The Hunky trainers weren't like anything she'd ever seen before. The front split into two sections, like a pig's foot, and the toes were covered with brown stains and smears.

STEP OUT OF YOUR STY!

said the poster.

GET INTO HUNKY TROTTERS!!

Harvey gazed longingly at them. 'Aren't they just — just IT? I bet they cost a fortune. D'you think Mum would buy some for me? If I promised to do all the washing up, for a year?'

'You've only just had new trainers,' said Lloyd. 'It's Dinah who needs some.' He looked enviously at her. 'Lucky beast.'

Harvey sidled up to Dinah. 'Your feet aren't *much*

bigger than mine, Di. Get Mum to buy you some of those Trotters. Then I can borrow them.'

Dinah looked at the Trotters and shuddered. They were *deformed*. How could anyone — ?

She was just opening her mouth to tell Harvey how much she hated them, when there was a yell from the school playground next door. It was followed by a shrill scream, and then a loud, steady chant. Stepping back from the shop window, Dinah caught the words.

'Hunky — or nothing! Hunky — or nothing!'

What on earth . . .?

Lloyd and Harvey heard it too. They dashed for the school gate, and Dinah followed, peering through the railings to see what was happening.

There was a huge crowd of children in one corner, all of them festooned with Hunky badges and scarves and bags. Through the crowd, Dinah glimpsed a small, terrified figure, dressed in neat school uniform. He was cowering back against the school wall, holding up an arm to protect his face.

The others pressed closer and closer, and the chant rose to a shout.

'HUNKY — OR NOTHING! HUNKY — OR NOTHING!'

Dinah raced into the playground and grabbed Alison Edwards, who was at the back of the crowd. 'What's going on? Why is everyone picking on Benedict?'

'Can't you *see*?' Alison said, scowling. 'He hasn't got

19

any Hunky things. And he says he doesn't know about Hunky!' She wrenched her arm away from Dinah and turned back, taking up the chant again in a fierce, jeering voice. 'HUNKY — OR NOTHING!'

Dinah's mouth fell open. She couldn't believe what was happening. For a second, she didn't know what to do. Then, to her horror, she heard two familiar voices, shouting right next to her.

'HUNKY — OR NOTHING!'

It was Lloyd and Harvey. They were both grinning, and yelling loudly, like everyone else. As if the whole thing were a great joke.

Dinah grabbed their arms, and shook them as hard as she could. 'Stop it!' she screamed. 'Don't be so horrible! Stop it this *minute*!'

Chapter 3

— or Nothing!

When Lloyd raced into the playground, he didn't know what was happening. He thought there must be a big fight going on, or some kind of argument.

Then he saw Benedict Watts, with the whole crowd round him.

Benedict Watts, in his silly, childish, SMUG school uniform, with not so much as a Hunky Parker badge on it.

Lloyd felt his face grow hot, and his heart began to thud in his chest. Angry thoughts buzzed round his mind, all by themselves, as though a small voice had whispered them into his ear.

It's people like that who spoil all the fun! People who won't join in! People who try to be clever! Suddenly, words started bursting out of his mouth, and he found himself chanting with everyone else.

'Hunky — or nothing!'

At exactly the same moment, Harvey started chanting too, and Lloyd grinned sideways at him. *We'll show them!* he thought. *We'll show people they can't try and stop us liking Hunky!* The two of them took a step forward and raised their voices, and Lloyd glared through the crowd at Benedict.

'HUNKY — OR NOTHING!'

21

And then Dinah grabbed them.

Lloyd hadn't given her a thought. He was totally caught up in the chant, and he wasn't looking at anything except the green of Benedict's school uniform. But suddenly there she was, with her fingers digging into his shoulder. She was nothing like as big as he was, but she shook him so hard that the words caught in his throat and he stopped yelling.

At the same moment, Benedict's voice rose over the noise of the crowd, in a shrill wail.

'But I *can't* watch Hunky Parker! It's on when I have my cello lesson!'

There was a loud, jeering roar from the crowd, but Lloyd and Harvey couldn't join in. Dinah shook them again and hissed furiously.

'You see? They're all picking on him, and it's *not his fault!* Is it?'

'I — ' Lloyd blinked and shook his head from side to side. Suddenly it felt muzzy.

Dinah was glaring at them. Her face had gone white with shock. 'What made you join in? You *never* bully people like that.'

'I — ' Lloyd was still struggling for words. He simply had no idea what had happened.

Harvey blinked up at Dinah. 'It was like . . . like being in a play or something. When I came in, I just knew what I had to do. As if I'd been told beforehand.'

'For goodness sake!' Dinah almost exploded. 'That's the most feeble excuse I ever heard!'

'But . . . but it *was* like that,' Lloyd said slowly. 'I looked at Benedict, and — it was just as if someone told me what to do.'

Dinah obviously didn't believe him. 'I didn't think you *let* other people tell you what to do. You're the person who's always giving orders.'

Lloyd's head cleared. She was right! He shouldn't be letting himself be pushed around by . . . by whatever it was. He should be —

'I'm going to stop this,' he said firmly. 'I'm going to get Benedict out of there.'

'*How?*' Harvey turned back to the crowd, and his voice wobbled and died away. The chant was louder than ever, and Benedict was pressed right back against the drain-pipe, so squashed that his schoolbag was being trodden underfoot.

Even Dinah looked daunted. 'What can we do? We can't fight off that many people.'

'We're not going to fight them,' Lloyd said. He raised his chin defiantly. 'We're going to make them see reason. At least, *I* am.'

'They won't listen to you!' wailed Harvey.

Lloyd didn't take any notice. He began to push his way into the crowd, digging his elbows in, and dragging people sideways, so that he could wriggle through. One or two children pushed back, but most of them didn't take any notice. They were concentrating on Benedict.

With a final, ferocious shove, Lloyd reached the front. Benedict's eyes widened in horror, as though he expected

23

some new kind of trouble, and Lloyd leaned forward and hissed in his ear.

'Don't worry. I'll get you out of this.'

Then he turned to face the crowd — and his heart almost stopped beating.

Scores of people were staring at him. Hundreds of angry, jeering eyes glared above fiercely chanting mouths. It was a dangerous, uncontrolled crowd.

He took a deep breath and bellowed as loudly as he could. 'Stop it! It's stupid! Leave him alone!'

Not a single person listened to him. But their eyes grew angrier, and suddenly the chant began to change. It grew sharper and shorter, and the crowd pressed forward, stretching out hands to pluck at Benedict's clothes.

'Nothing! Nothing! Nothing!'

The word sliced through the air like an ugly steel blade, dangerous and threatening. Lloyd could feel the tension building up, and he knew he hadn't got much time left. He had to get them all to change their minds, or he would find himself in a hopelessly uneven fight. With him and Benedict on one side, and the rest of the school on the other. He had to talk himself out of it.

But how? Lloyd looked sideways at Benedict and almost despaired. He was so . . . so *Hunkyless*. He hadn't got a single Hunky thing anywhere on his clothes or in his bag. If only —

That was it! Desperately, moving so fast that his hands stumbled and the pin pricked his fingers, Lloyd

24

unpinned the bright new Hunky Parker badge he was wearing on his school coat.

He had no time to explain what he was doing. He simply grabbed Benedict, pinned the badge on to the front of his green blazer and spun him round to face the crowd.

It worked like magic. Almost immediately, the shouting voices died away, and people began to fall back, looking rather foolish. Lloyd grinned at them, over Benedict's head.

'Who's always right?' he yelled.

That stopped them feeling stupid. The answer came back, in a final, joyful bellow.

'HUNKY PARKER!'

Then they turned and began straggling away into school. Dinah and Harvey pushed their way towards Lloyd.

'That was swilliant, L!' Harvey said. 'You're a genius.'

Lloyd tried to look modest. 'Just lucky.' He glanced at Benedict. 'You OK, Ben?'

'I . . . I . . .' Benedict was still shaking. 'It w-wasn't my fault. I d-didn't mean to upset them. I didn't d-do anything. Thanks, Lloyd.'

'That's all right,' Lloyd said, airily. 'I think you'll be safe now. But you'd better go on wearing that Hunky Parker badge for the time being.'

Benedict looked down at it, and pulled a disgusted face. 'Do I *have* to?'

For a second, Lloyd heard the small voice whispering in his head again. *It's people like that who spoil all the fun!* He struggled to ignore it, but he could feel the smile disappearing from his face.

'Why don't you watch the programme?' he said coldly. 'Then you'd understand why we all like Hunky.'

'But it's the day I have my cello lesson — '

Lloyd screwed up his fists. 'OK. Don't go on about it. Stick with your wretched cello lesson if you want to. But make sure you wear the badge. *And look as though you like it.*'

'Yes. Of course. Thanks a lot.' Picking up his dusty, battered schoolbag, Benedict scuttled into the building.

Dinah grinned at Lloyd. 'Well done.'

But Harvey wasn't smiling. He looked down at his feet, scuffing them along the playground.

'What's the matter, H?' Lloyd frowned at him. 'Aren't you pleased I got Benedict out?'

'Yes, of course I am,' muttered Harvey.

'So?'

'So . . . ' Harvey hesitated. 'It sounds silly.'

Lloyd sighed, but Dinah was watching Harvey's face. 'We won't laugh,' she said quietly. 'Tell us what's the matter.'

Harvey shuffled his feet again. 'It's — well — you know when we first heard them shouting? When we were outside, by the shoe shop?'

Dinah nodded.

'Well — just *before* I heard the words, I had a very strange feeling. As if — ' Harvey glanced from Dinah to Lloyd and back again. ' — as if I *knew* what they were, without hearing them. And I *had* to join in.'

Dinah looked puzzled. 'But you didn't *have* to. Nobody made you.'

Lloyd felt as though a cold finger had touched his chest. 'I know what he means,' he said slowly. 'Because I knew too. And it wasn't just *then* that I felt I had to shout. Just now — when Ben was saying he couldn't watch Hunky Parker — I felt really cross with him.'

'But that's ridiculous!' Dinah swallowed. 'You know what Ben's like. He never watches *anything* on television. And why does it matter, anyway?'

Lloyd shook his head, trying to make sense of it all. 'I don't know. I just feel — as though *everything* has to be Hunky Parker.'

'Well, you won't get me watching it!' Dinah said. 'I may wear the T-shirt, but I'm not going to waste my time on the programme.'

'Of course not,' Lloyd said quickly.

But, for one, sickening moment, he found himself thinking *Hunky — or nothing!* And when he looked across at Harvey, he saw that his fists were clenched.

Chapter 4

Dinah's Birthday

Dinah thought the Benedict business would put the others off Hunky Parker. She was wrong. They were quiet and shaken for a day or two — but only until the next programme. Then they were as Hunky-mad as ever. Dinah began to spend more and more time in her bedroom, because it was the only way to escape.

Well, I'm not having a Hunky birthday party, anyway, she thought. She shook her head politely when Mrs Hunter suggested a pig cake.

'I'd rather have it iced like a calculator. If you don't mind.'

Mrs Hunter didn't argue. 'Well, if you're sure . . .'

But, on the day of the party, she looked regretfully at the tea table.

'A Hunky Parker cake would have been more striking.'

'It's lovely like this,' Dinah said, firmly. She looked at the sandwiches and little sausages, the biscuits with clown faces on, and the little chocolate cakes. 'A real family birthday party. Thank you, Mum.'

She hugged Mrs Hunter, and then went off to open the front door, to let in Ingrid and Ian and Mandy.

Ingrid was bouncing, holding something flat and rectangular. 'Wait till you see what I've got! I've been waiting for them to come on sale here.'

Lloyd and Harvey came racing down the stairs.

'Go on, Di!' said Lloyd. 'Open it.'

Dinah looked down. The shape of the parcel looked frighteningly familiar. She had a nasty feeling —

'Go *on*!' Harvey was getting impatient.

Dinah undid the Sellotape and took off the paper. She swallowed. It was a Hunky Parker video.

'Thanks,' she said stiffly.

Harvey goggled. 'Where did you *find* it, Ing?'

'They've just come into the shops,' Ingrid said. 'This morning.' She hopped down the hall on one foot, grinning all over her face. 'You'll love it! It's *swilliant*!'

'My present's even better,' drawled Ian, holding out a long roll. 'Here you are.'

Dinah undid the string and the roll unwound itself suddenly, slithering about in her hands. There, staring up at her, was a vast picture of — Hunky Parker. With every disgusting detail larger than life.

'Honey-coloured hamburgers!' yelled Lloyd. 'That's fantastic!'

Ian smiled, modestly. 'You can stick it over your bed, Di. Then it'll be the first thing you see, when you wake up.'

Dinah could just imagine it. She made herself smile again. 'Thanks very much.'

'Now Mandy's!' Harvey was really enjoying himself.

30

As Dinah took Mandy's parcel, he pushed closer to her, so he could be the first to see what was inside.

'I hope you like it,' Mandy said. 'I made it myself.'

That didn't sound like Hunky Parker. Dinah grinned at her, slipped off the paper — and froze.

'Now that is ED-u-cated,' murmured Ian. 'Really takes you out of your sty, doesn't it?'

Dinah was speechless. Inside the parcel was a pyjama case in the shape of Hunky Parker. Dirt and all. There was even a grey satin lining to the snout, to make it look really slimy. *I'll die if I have to put my pyjamas in that*, she thought.

But she smiled again. 'That's wonderful, Mandy. Thanks. I — Let's play some games, shall we? Lloyd's got a list.'

With a nod, Lloyd began to organize everyone.

'We're going in the garden. Did you bring your trainers, like I told you to?'

'Sure did.' Ingrid stood on her head and waggled her feet in the air.

Lloyd waved a hand. 'Get ours out then, H.'

Harvey went to rummage in the cupboard under the stairs. After a few moments, he stuck his head out, frowning.

'I can't see Dinah's.'

Mrs Hunter came out of the dining-room. 'That's because I've sent her old ones to the jumble sale. Hang on.' She pulled a carrier bag out of the cupboard and handed it to Dinah. 'I hope these are all right.'

Dinah had a terrible, sinking feeling. She slid her hand into the bag, and pulled out — a pair of Hunky Trotters.

It was the last straw. She dropped them on the floor, put her face in her hands and burst into tears.

'What's up with you?' said Harvey. '*I* wouldn't be crying if *I* had a pair of Trotters.'

Mrs Hunter picked them up and looked helplessly at them. 'There wasn't any point in asking if you liked them, Dinah. There's nothing else in the shops. I *had* to buy Trotters.'

'I . . . I . . . ' Dinah tried to stop crying, but she couldn't. It was awful. She just went on and on sobbing.

'What's the matter?' said Ingrid, turning the right way up again. 'Don't you *like* Hunky Parker, Di?'

Mandy looked horrified. 'Why didn't you say?'

'It's her own fault,' Lloyd muttered crossly. 'She's never watched any of the programmes. She doesn't understand about Hunky.'

'Well, we can soon change *that*!' Ingrid beamed and picked up the video she had just given Dinah. 'Come on.'

It's my birthday, thought Dinah. *And I don't want to watch a Hunky Parker video*. But how could she refuse?

'All right,' she said, in a small, tight voice.

Mrs Hunter smiled and went off to the kitchen, and the others hustled Dinah into the sitting-room. They were eager, even if she wasn't. In a few seconds, they were all sitting down, staring at the television screen.

'Ready?' said Lloyd. He pressed the button on the

remote control and there was Hunky Parker, leering at them.

'Ready, everyone?' he said, in his horrible, smug voice. 'This'll take you out of your sty and plaster you all over the road. So don't even *blink*, in case you miss something.'

Yuck! thought Dinah. *Yuck, yuck, YUCK!!* But she forced herself to keep watching as Hunky waddled towards a shop full of wedding dresses. It didn't take much to guess what was going to happen. She tried not to shudder.

And then her brain twitched.

That was the only way to describe it. One second she was thinking *Yuck!* and the next she was thinking *Hunky's all right really. Quite . . . quite . . .*

She went very still and stiff in her chair, fighting the feeling. Her mind couldn't change. Not on its own. Not for no *reason*.

Then it happened again. Hunky began smearing mud down the wedding dresses — and suddenly she thought, *Maybe those Trotters are worth having.*

No! She couldn't bear it! She had to stop the video! Grabbing the remote control from Lloyd's lap, she stabbed at it with her finger and the picture on the screen froze. Dinah sighed with relief.

But only for a second. Then she was staring at the screen again, completely baffled.

The picture that was frozen there didn't seem to belong to the video at all.

33

* * *

'Orange ostrich eggs! What are you *doing*?' Lloyd reached for the remote control — and then stopped, with a frown. 'What's that?'

'It's not on the video,' Ingrid said, in a puzzled voice. 'I watched it all the way through, before I wrapped it up, and I didn't see that.'

Frozen on the screen was a picture of Hunky Parker. The familiar dirty, slobbering face stared out at them, just as it stared out from their T-shirts and from a hundred things they saw every day. But it wasn't a cartoon any more.

It was a mask.

And, through the mask, cold, sea-green eyes were staring at them.

They were glittering, riveting eyes. Dinah felt them drilling into her head, branding the pig's image on her brain so that she couldn't get rid of it.

Below the face was a card, with three words painted on it, in clear, black letters.

HUNKY — OR NOTHING!

'Go on with the video,' Lloyd said harshly. 'Let's see what comes next.'

Dinah picked up the remote control again and pressed Play. Instantly, they were back in the wedding dress shop, watching Hunky trampling white satin under his trotters.

She shivered.

34

'Go back,' Lloyd said. 'Freeze that frame again.'

Dinah tried. Three times she pressed the button too late, and froze pictures of Hunky in the wedding dress shop. But the fourth time she hit it at exactly the right instant. There was the masked figure again, with the same notice.

And the same icy, unblinking eyes.

Harvey wriggled in his chair. 'I don't understand. You've just been straight past this bit, without stopping. Why didn't we see this picture then? When the video was running.'

'I think . . . there wasn't time,' Dinah said slowly, working it out as she spoke. 'It must be just a single frame.'

'You mean it flashed past too fast for us to see?' Mandy looked puzzled. 'What's the point of that?'

'Oh, we saw it all right.' Dinah swallowed. She remembered, exactly, the terrifying way her mind had obeyed the picture. 'But we didn't *know* we'd seen it. And — wait a minute.'

She rewound the video, to the place where Hunky was going into the wedding dress shop. That was where her brain had twitched first. Where she had started to think *Hunky's all right really*. And somewhere there . . .

It took her longer to find the hidden frame this time, because she wasn't sure exactly where to look. But none of the others complained as she flicked the video backwards and forwards, on and off. They were all concentrating on the screen.

At last she hit it. The same frame, with the masked figure holding the black and white notice.

And the same paralysing eyes.

'It's stupid!' Ingrid glared uncomfortably at the screen. 'What's the use of putting in pictures that no one knows about? Who's going to take any notice of that?'

'You might not take any notice now you know about it,' murmured Ian. 'But when it was hidden —'

'Subliminal,' Dinah said, in a hard, angry voice. 'That's what they call it. It's a subliminal frame. Meant

to put things into people's minds without letting them realize it.'

Lloyd stared at the screen. 'Do you think,' he said slowly, 'that there are other frames like that? Maybe — on the TV programmes?'

'I'm sure there are,' Dinah said.

'So we've been tricked?' Lloyd looked away from the masked face. 'Is that why I felt so angry with Benedict for not liking Hunky Parker?'

'That's why you liked Hunky Parker in the first place!' Dinah said fiercely. 'Don't you remember? None of you could stand him, until you saw Ingrid's video. I bet that's chockful of subliminal frames.'

'To make people want Hunky Parker things,' Mandy said.

Dinah nodded. 'Anything with that face on.' She frowned at the screen. 'If you watch Hunky Parker, you'll do whatever that . . . that *monster* tells you.'

Ian looked stunned, but Ingrid went red in the face. 'I don't believe it!' she said stubbornly. 'I don't like Hunky because of some freaky thing on your video. I like him because he's *nice*.'

'OK,' Dinah said quietly. 'Go and get *your* video, and we'll have a look at that.'

Twenty minutes later, they were staring at the masked face again, but this time it was on Ingrid's video. And she was as horrified as everyone else.

'We've got to phone the police,' she said grimly. 'To tell them the Hunky Parker people are tricking everyone.'

Lloyd didn't usually take orders from Ingrid, but this time he jumped up straight away. The others crowded round the telephone as he found the number of the police station and dialled.

The moment someone answered, he began talking. 'I want to make a complaint about a Hunky Parker video.'

There was a deep chuckle from the other end. 'Ah, an ED-u-cated complaint! And what's the matter with your video?'

'It's got — ' Lloyd put his hand over the mouthpiece and hissed at Dinah. 'What's it called?'

'Subliminal frames.'

'Subliminal frames,' Lloyd repeated, into the telephone. 'You can't see them, unless you freeze them — at least, you do but you don't know — and they . . . they make you want to buy Hunky Parker things. You can't help yourself.'

The voice chuckled again. 'That's the excuse you're giving your mother, is it? *Swilliant*, sonny. Wish I'd thought of it myself.'

'No!' Lloyd said, desperately. 'I'm not joking. This is serious.'

'Hmm.'

The policeman paused for a moment, and Lloyd bit his tongue. *Please listen!* he wanted to yell. *You've got to listen!* But he made himself wait.

38

'Tell you what,' the policeman said at last, 'I'm going off duty now, but I wouldn't mind taking a look at your video. How about bringing it in tomorrow afternoon?'

'Wednesday?' Lloyd said. 'Great! We'll come after school!'

'I'll make a note of it, then. What's your name and address?'

Lloyd told him, and said goodbye. As he put the phone down, he heard the policeman chuckle again. He was speaking to someone at the other end of the line. 'Just heard a good one. About a Hunky Parker video . . .'

Ingrid heard it too. She frowned. 'He thinks it's funny.'

'So?' Ian shrugged. 'He'll change his mind when he sees the video. He can say what he likes till then.'

Lloyd nodded, but Dinah had a strange, uneasy feeling.

She wished she knew who had been listening to the policeman's joke.

Chapter 5

Gone!

The moment school was over next day, they all raced back to the Hunters' house, to fetch the videos. Harvey was first into the sitting-room. He looked along the row of videos on the shelf and frowned. Then he knelt down and pressed Eject.

Nothing slid out of the machine.

Lloyd frowned. 'Where's your video, Di? Did you take it upstairs?'

Dinah shook her head. 'I didn't touch it. And what about Ingrid's? That ought to be here too.'

Lloyd checked the video shelf again, but there was no Hunky Parker video. 'Mum must have moved them. I'll go and ask her.'

But when he went into the kitchen, Mrs Hunter shook her head. 'You know I always leave the videos alone. That machine's beyond me.'

'What about Dad?'

'He didn't even go in there. He came in late and went straight to bed.'

Lloyd felt as though someone had laid an icy finger on the back of his neck. The others were drifting into the kitchen, but he didn't have time to explain. He had to find out what had happened.

'Has anyone else been here?'

Mrs Hunter looked puzzled. 'No, I don't think so. Only the man to service the television. Why do you — ?'

'*The man to service the television?*' Dinah said. 'What do you mean? *No one* services the television.'

'I . . . Oh.' Mrs Hunter stopped, and frowned. 'I suppose you're right. But I was busy, and he had an identity card. And brown overalls with a badge, like a uniform. So I didn't think . . . What's all this about, anyway?'

Harvey went pink. 'He wasn't a *real* television man! He came to steal Dinah's video. And Ingrid's.'

Mrs Hunter stared for a moment. Then she began to laugh. '*Harvey!* What a load of nonsense. How could he have known the videos were here? Anyway, I can't see what all the fuss is about. I thought Dinah hated Hunky Parker.'

She shooed them out of the kitchen, and they stood in the hall, staring at each other. None of them could quite believe what had happened.

'Do you think it was . . . the policeman?' faltered Harvey. 'He was the only person we told.'

'But *he* told other people,' Lloyd said, grimly. 'I bet he told everyone who walked into the police station last night. And one of those people must have been the man in brown overalls. Or someone connected with him.'

'What does it matter who it was?' drawled Ian. 'If we haven't got the video, no one's going to believe us. We can't do anything.'

41

'We've *got* to do something,' Lloyd said stubbornly. 'We can't just give up.'

For a second they stared at each other. Then Dinah turned and ran upstairs. When she came down, she was carrying her money box.

'Right,' she said, in a quiet, angry voice. 'We're going to the shops.'

Harvey looked puzzled. 'But that's your computer money, Di. You've been saving up for *months*.'

'Computers can wait,' Dinah said. 'Right now, what I want most in the world is another Hunky Parker video. Come on!'

They went to Woolworths first, because it was nearest. But as soon as they walked through the door, they could see that there was something peculiar going on.

The walls were plastered with advertisements for The Sty (The ED-u-cated holiday! Sun tomorrow, snow today!) and all round them were shelves crammed with Hunky Parker things. Clothes and sweets and pictures and toys. The sort of stuff that people were usually fighting to buy.

But no one was paying any attention to those. Everyone in the shop had crowded round the video shelves, and angry voices were shouting backwards and forwards. Old ladies waved their umbrellas, children wailed, and men in smart suits banged their fists on the counter.

'It's no use hanging around here,' Dinah said quickly. 'We can't even *see* the videos. Let's go somewhere else.'

She led the way out of the shop before Lloyd had a chance to argue, and walked along to Smith's.

But that was just the same. Hunky Parker pens and notebooks and calculators were standing untouched, and there was a huge crowd of people at the far end of the shop, where the videos were kept.

This crowd was even uglier than the one in Woolworths. People were beginning to stamp their feet, and some of them were shouting, 'We want the Manager!'

Lloyd felt uneasy. 'Something's up, isn't it? D'you think it could have anything to do with the man in brown overalls?'

'We haven't got time to chat,' Dinah said grimly. 'We can do that afterwards. When we've got a video. Come on.'

She marched out of the shop, and the others had to follow her. But Lloyd hung behind, glancing over his shoulder. He could hear the chant changing behind him, and he knew what the crowd was saying, even before he made out the words.

'Hunky — or nothing! Hunky — or nothing!'

With a shudder, he ran out of the shop and chased after the others. He didn't know what was causing all the trouble, but he didn't like the sound of that crowd.

Dinah was heading for the little bookshop at the bottom of the hill. Mrs French, the bookseller, wouldn't have anything to do with television, but she stocked one

43

or two videos, on a stand at the back of the shop. Lloyd was sure the Hunky Parker one would be there.

But it wasn't.

They could see that, as soon as they pushed open the shop door. The video stand was completely empty.

When Lloyd caught sight of it, he felt his face go red and his heart start to thud. *Fancy not having any Hunky videos!* whispered a little voice in his head. *It's disgusting! They should have Hunky. Hunky — or nothing! Hunky —*

And, like an echo, two voices spoke right in front of him.

'She *should* have it!' said Mandy.

'Hunky — or nothing!' snapped Ingrid.

'No!' Lloyd clenched his fists. 'Can't you see what's happening to you? It's the subliminal frames!'

Mandy went white, and Ingrid clapped her hands over her mouth. In the sudden silence, they heard more voices coming from round the corner, where Mrs French had her office.

'You think we're idiots? We know that video's out!'

'If you haven't got any, you'll have to *get some*!'

'Hunky — or nothing!'

Lloyd and Dinah looked at each other. Dinah nodded, and Lloyd led the way up the shop to the office. Mrs French was sitting behind her desk, cowering backwards as three teenage boys loomed over her, shouting furiously.

'I can't *help* it!' she said, plaintively. 'People keep coming in and asking for Hunky videos, but there's nothing I can do. I did have some in yesterday, but the van came round this morning and took them away.'

The tallest boy growled at her. 'Took them *all* away?'

'The delivery man said they were faulty,' Mrs French said. '*I* haven't had any complaints, but that didn't make any difference. He refunded my money — and he took every one.'

The tall boy leaned forward and grabbed the collar of her blouse. 'Then you'll have to order some more, won't you?' he said nastily. 'Right away!'

'Oh, I have! I have already!' Mrs French picked up a piece of paper and flapped it desperately under his nose. 'But he said they couldn't deliver them for at least a week.'

'Then you'll have to go and *get* them, won't you?' The boy began to shake her. 'Where do they come from?'

'I'm not — ' Mrs French started to choke as her collar tightened. 'I'm not allowed to tell. I had to sign a contract — '

Lloyd glanced sideways at Dinah and the others. SPLAT couldn't just stand there while Mrs French got beaten up. He'd have to give them an order.

But, before he could think of the right order to give, there was a noise from outside. A steady, rhythmic shouting, and the sound of tramping feet. It sounded as though a lot of people were coming down the hill.

The three boys let go of Mrs French and pushed past Lloyd and the others, hurrying towards the door. Mandy ran into the office.

'Are you all right, Mrs French? Do you need any help?'

'I — no thank you, dear. I'm just a bit shaken up. I knew I was in for trouble, the moment the delivery man walked in this morning and I saw his brown overall. He — What *is* that noise?'

She got to her feet, looking rather wobbly, and made for the doorway. The three boys were still blocking it, but suddenly they gave a great whoop and charged out. Lloyd followed Mrs French to the door and looked up the hill.

He could hardly believe his eyes.

There was a huge crowd, marching down towards them, filling the whole road. And from the crowd came a steady chant, keeping pace with the marching feet.

'HUNKY — OR NOTHING! HUNKY — OR NOTHING!'

Mrs French swallowed. 'It's . . . it's like an army. What do they want?'

Dinah twisted her hands together. 'They're making sure all the shops keep stocking Hunky Parker goods,' she said, in a small, tight voice. 'No one will *dare* to run out now.'

Mrs French didn't listen. She stood up very straight,

making a sudden decision. 'Well, they're not coming in *here*. I'm going to shut the shop. I'll have to turn you all out.'

Mandy looked nervously up the hill. 'We'd better go quickly, then. We don't want to get mixed up with *them*. Where's Ingrid?'

Ingrid was sauntering up from the back of the shop, with her hands in her pockets. *Typical*, thought Lloyd. But he didn't waste time telling her off for being awkward. He grabbed her arm and pushed her out of the shop in front of him.

As Mrs French locked the door behind them, they ran down the road and round the first corner, and then stopped, to watch the huge crowd go past. It was an awe-inspiring sight. There must have been several hundred people, all marching and chanting together.

'It's . . . it's just like Mrs French said,' stuttered Harvey. 'They're like an *army*.'

Dinah nodded grimly. 'And what I'd like to know is — who's giving them orders? Where does all this Hunky Parker stuff come from?'

'We'll never find that out,' said Lloyd, with his eyes still on the crowd. 'Didn't you hear what Mrs French said? The shopkeepers aren't allowed to tell. We've lost your video, and we haven't got a hope of tracking down another one.'

'Oh yes, we have!' said Ingrid.

She sounded so smug that they all turned round to

48

look at her. Pulling a tiny, torn scrap of paper out of her pocket, she waved it under their noses.

'It's a good thing *someone's* got some brains!'

Ian blinked. 'That's your brains?'

Ingrid kicked him. 'It's the address Mrs French orders her Hunky videos from!' She waved it again, triumphantly. 'I ripped off the corner of the paper while you were all gazing out of the door.'

Lloyd leaned forward and read the address. 'It's *miles* away.'

'It wouldn't take very long on the train,' Dinah said thoughtfully. 'Only a couple of hours.'

'But think what it would cost.' Mandy sighed. 'And we've spent all the SPLAT savings on those stupid T-shirts. How can we go?'

Dinah shook her money box. 'I've got enough in here. We can go tomorrow.'

'What about school?' said Harvey.

Dinah stuck up her chin. She looked very pale and determined. 'We'll go first thing in the morning. Before school starts.'

'Mum won't let us,' said Lloyd.

'Then we'll go even earlier than *that*,' Dinah said fiercely. 'Before she's up. Don't you see? There's something terrible going on, and no one knows except us. We've *got* to do something about it!'

Chapter 6

Parker Products Ltd.

It was still dark when Dinah, Lloyd, and Harvey left home the next morning. They took their packed lunches and left a note propped on top of the fridge.

Gone on a special outing. Sorry we didn't tell you about it before. Love, L, H, & D.

They met the others at the station and caught a very early train. It was still before nine o'clock when they got off at the other end.

'But how will we find the *factory*?' Harvey had been getting more and more anxious all the way. 'We haven't got a map.'

'We'll ask,' Lloyd said. He marched briskly up to the barrier, waving the scrap of paper with the address on it.

The ticket collector looked at the name of the road and grinned. 'No problem. Turn left outside the station, then second right and first left and you're there.'

But he shook his head when they mentioned Hunky Parker.

'Never heard of anything like that round here. It's all DIY and carpet showrooms. I wouldn't mind, though. I like that Hunky Parker.'

'You do?' Mandy said faintly.

'Got ED-u-cated socks, haven't I?'

Pulling up his trouser-legs, the ticket collector did a little dance. There, leering up from his ankles, was Hunky Parker's face.

Dinah shuddered. The more she saw that face, the worse she felt. 'Let's get on.'

Lloyd nodded. They were all feeling nervous, but it was no use wasting time. 'SPLAT — forward!'

He led the way out of the station, following the directions they had been given.

Dinah trailed a little behind, puzzling over what the ticket collector had said. Why hadn't he heard of the factory? If all the Hunky Parker things were made there, it must be enormous. And surely it would be bright, as well. She could just imagine the slogans painted across the front.

PARKER PRODUCTS ARE SWILLIANT!!!
HUNKY — OR NOTHING!!!

Or just a giant pig's face, maybe, staring down from over the door. But there was sure to be something striking about it.

Lloyd must have been looking for somewhere like that too, because he led them right past the place. Dinah suddenly realized they were outside number ninety-six.

'Hey, stop!' she called softly. 'Eighty-four's back this way.'

She turned and began to walk back, counting the

numbers carefully as she went. Ninety-four, ninety-two, ninety . . .

Even then, she almost missed it. The numbers seemed to go straight from eighty-six, which was a big carpet warehouse, to eighty-two, which was a kitchen showroom. Dinah stopped outside and peered down the gap in between.

There, set back from the road, was a narrow grey building. It had a small door, but no windows at the front. There was no notice either, except for a small brass plate beside the door.

The others were still on their way back, but Dinah didn't wait for them. Slipping down the alley, she went to read the brass plate. It said, Parker Products Ltd.

Trembling slightly, she walked back to meet the others. 'This is the place,' she murmured.

'But — ' Lloyd stared. 'It can't be. They can't make *anything* in there. There's no room.'

'Perhaps this isn't the factory,' said Mandy. 'Maybe it's just the place that sends things to the shops.'

Ingrid was getting impatient. 'Why are we wasting time *talking*? If we want to know what's going on, we ought to ask. I'll go and knock on the door.'

'*No!*' Dinah grabbed her sleeve, just in time. 'We mustn't let them know we're here. Not until we've seen what kind of place it is.'

'What are we going to do, then?' Ingrid looked sulky. 'Stand out here, staring?'

Lloyd decided it was time to take charge. 'We'll go

round the back. There's a side road just past the carpet place. Let's try that.'

Turning down the side road, they found a car-park behind the carpet warehouse. And further down the road, beyond the car-park, was a small, narrow alley, just wide enough for a lorry to drive through.

Lloyd took a deep breath. 'I bet that alley leads to Parker Products.'

'We'll have to go and look,' Dinah said. Her heart was thudding, but there was no way out. Now they'd come so far, they had to find out what they could.

'Race you!' said Ingrid boldly, but Mandy grabbed her arm.

'Don't! We've got to be *careful*, Ing.'

Ingrid snorted. 'It's no use being scared. We've got to find out what's going on. Come on.'

It was dark and damp in the alley. On one side was the back fence of the car-park and on the other was a row of tall, dripping trees. Dinah pulled her coat more tightly round her and made sure she kept up with the others.

They came out into a concrete yard, surrounded by a high brick wall. Standing in the yard were a dozen plain grey lorries with three words painted on their sides in small, neat letters: Parker Products Ltd.

There was no one around, but large, grimy windows looked down from the back of the Parker Products building. Mandy shuddered and pulled Ingrid back into the shelter of the fence.

'Suppose they look out and see us?'

Dinah studied the windows. 'I don't think they can. Not while we're up in this corner. But we can't see much either.'

'We haven't come sight-seeing,' murmured Ian. 'All we need is one little video. There are probably some in those lorries, if we only knew.' He smiled a slow, teasing smile. 'Who's brave enough to go and look?'

He meant it as a joke, but Ingrid didn't leave anyone time to laugh.

'Me!' she said.

Before anyone could stop her, she had darted out of the shelter of the alley, and was half-way to the nearest lorry.

'Ingrid!' Mandy would have followed, but Dinah held her back.

'It's *more* dangerous if you go too,' she hissed. 'They're more likely to notice two people than one.'

They stood and watched Ingrid creeping from one lorry to another. She kept looking up, nervously, at the big windows, but no face appeared behind the grimy glass and she crept on and on. She was heading for the furthest lorry, which had its back doors wide open.

'Oh hurry!' whispered Mandy, under her breath. 'Don't let them catch you.'

Reaching the lorry, Ingrid hesitated for a moment, peering in. Then she clambered up and disappeared inside. The others stared at the black opening, waiting for her to reappear.

But she didn't.

'It's my fault,' Mandy said, wretchedly. 'I should never have let go of her hand. I'll go and fetch her back.'

'I'm smaller than you,' Dinah said quickly. Mandy was much too upset to be careful. 'I'll go.'

Not giving herself time to think about it, she glanced up at the empty windows and then ran towards the first lorry. She worked her way along the line, just as Ingrid had done, and peered into the open doors at the end.

The lorry was full of big wooden crates. Ingrid was up at the front, rummaging in one of them, and Dinah called softly.

'Ing! What are you doing?'

'Checking,' hissed Ingrid. 'Most of these boxes are empty, but there might be videos in one of them.'

Dinah looked at the dark inside of the lorry and thought about being trapped in there. But she had to get Ingrid out. She hauled herself up and clambered in.

'I'll give you a hand, but we must *hurry*.'

She crept between the crates, reading the words on them as her eyes grew used to the dark.

READY-DRIBBLED BABYWEAR!

said one.

FOR ED-U-CATED PIGLETS!!

Above the words was a picture of a fat baby in a babysuit with Hunky Parker's face on the front. All round the face were smears and blobs, like splattered food.

Yuck! thought Dinah. She crept up to Ingrid and whispered in her ear. 'Which crates are left to look in?'

Ingrid was just turning round to show her, when there

55

was an enormous yell from the far side of the car-park, where they had left the others.

'STOP!'

For a second, Dinah froze. Someone had seen them climbing into the lorry! Someone was coming to get them!

Then there was another yell, and this time the voice was familiar.

'OUCH! Let me go! You're hurting me!'

'Harvey!' hissed Ingrid. She turned to run out of the van, but Dinah caught her just in time.

'Don't be silly! Let's find out what's going on first.'

The two of them tiptoed down to the end and peered out, very cautiously. For a moment they couldn't see anything, except the other lorries. Then Harvey came staggering out from behind one, struggling in the arms of a tall man in brown overalls.

'What's wrong with the others?' Ingrid muttered furiously. 'Why aren't they rescuing him?'

She soon found out. Three other men in brown overalls followed the first one. They were dragging Lloyd and Mandy and Ian, keeping them quiet with hands jammed over their faces.

They pulled the four children into a row and stood perfectly still, waiting for something. For a few seconds, Dinah wondered if there was any point in charging out at them and trying to catch them off balance, but then there was another sound.

The *clip clip clip* of metal heels coming across the concrete.

'Well?' said a woman. 'Did you get them?'

The voice was sharp and mean, and the woman looked the same. She was wearing grey overalls and spiky high heels, and her hair was twisted into a tight little bun. When she saw the four prisoners, her eyes narrowed.

'What were you up to?' she snapped. 'What were you going to steal?'

'Nothing!' Harvey wriggled his mouth free and yelled at her. 'We're not thieves. And we wouldn't want anything to do with Hunky Parker!'

Oh, you IDIOT! thought Dinah. *Don't say anything else!*

The woman was suddenly very still. 'You don't want anything to do with Hunky? Why is that then?'

She was watching Harvey's face, very closely. Dinah shivered. *Be careful, Harvey!*

But Harvey was too cross and frightened to be careful. Turning purple in the face, he screeched up at the woman. 'Because Hunky Parker's horrible. I know how you tricked people into buying all those Hunky Parker things!'

The woman's eyes snapped. 'Do you now?' she said quietly. Her voice was very cold. She turned to the men in brown overalls and started giving orders. 'Tie them up. Put them in a lorry — *and take them to The Sty!*'

Suddenly, the men were very still. Dinah saw them look at each other.

'Oh, come on,' said one. 'They're only kids. Couldn't we just give them a clip round the ear and send them home?'

'Certainly not!' snapped the woman. 'We don't know what they've seen, and nothing must go wrong now. It's nearly time for HP9.'

'But — '

The woman drew herself up. '*What does Hunky say?*'

Peering out of the end of the van, Dinah could see all four of the men. As the woman spoke, their faces changed. Their eyes glazed over, and they chanted back at her, in a steady, mechanical singsong. '*Hunky says no snooping.*'

'That's right!' the woman said silkily. 'All snoopers have to be sent to The Sty. For a little talk with Hunky. Now get on with it!'

She stood with her arms folded, watching as first Lloyd and Harvey and then Ian and Mandy were gagged and trussed up in one of the vans. When they were all in, she nodded.

'On your way! You ought to be in Wales before lunch time.'

Wales? Ingrid's mouth fell open, but she was too horrified to speak. Dinah's brain whirled. They had no hope of getting the others free on their own, but they could get in touch with the police. Especially if they had the registration number of the lorry.

She leaned out as far as she dared, watching the men close up the heavy doors to shut the others in. She couldn't quite see the number, but when the van swung round, into the alley, there would be a very good view.

Maybe there was, but she didn't see it. As one of the men walked round to the front, to start the lorry up, the Grey Lady turned impatiently to the other three.

'Don't just hang around watching. Close up that end lorry and get all of them on the road.'

That end lorry . . . Just in time, Dinah realized what the woman meant. Grabbing Ingrid's shoulder, she pulled her back, behind the crates. They were only just out of sight when the doorway was filled by a tall figure in brown overalls.

BANG!

CLANG!

The doors crashed together, plunging the inside of the van into darkness. Ingrid's hand slid into Dinah's.

'Where d'you think we're going?' she said, in a small voice.

'I think . . . we're off to The Sty,' whispered Dinah. 'You know, that holiday place, in Wales. I think all the lorries are going there.'

'To The Sty?' Ingrid muttered. 'I don't understand.'

Dinah squeezed her hand. 'Don't worry. We're following the others. That's the main thing. We'll rescue them — *and* sort out Hunky Parker.'

As their lorry started, she stared into the darkness, wondering how on earth they were going to manage it.

Chapter 7

The Welcome Suite

Lloyd sat in the lorry, with the ropes biting into his wrists and ankles, and tried not to panic.

Dinah and Ingrid must have heard what was going on. Surely they'd go straight to the police! And then the police would come storming into The Sty to rescue them. And everything would be all right.

It *had* to be! Dinah and Ingrid had to *make* the police come!

But suppose they couldn't . . . ?

Lloyd closed his eyes as he remembered the Grey Lady's icy voice. *Take them to The Sty*, she had said. And the men in brown overalls had looked horrified. As if — as if —

The subliminal frame from the video danced behind Lloyd's eyelids. The image of the figure in the pig mask. The person with the terrible eyes — who *was* Hunky Parker.

Were they going to meet *him*?

All the way down the motorway, Lloyd avoided Harvey's frightened face. There was nothing he could do to cheer him up. They just had to wait and see what happened when they reached The Sty.

It was several hours before they turned off the motorway. By then, the journey was almost over. For twenty minutes or so the lorry turned left and right, along narrow, twisting lanes, sending Lloyd and the others sliding from side to side. Then it bumped over a couple of humps in the road and rattled up a steep hill.

They stopped at the top and, almost immediately, the big back doors were flung open.

'Take them to the Welcome Suite,' said a sharp voice.

For a second, Lloyd thought it was the Grey Lady from Parker Products. Then he saw that this one was taller. But she was wearing exactly the same clothes, and she was just as impatient.

'Get a move on!' she said briskly, as the men in brown overalls appeared. 'The weather is due to change in sixty-eight minutes, and these four have to be ready for that.'

The weather? How could they be that sure about the weather?

The men climbed into the van and seized Lloyd roughly. Dragging him to the back, they tossed him out on to the ground.

'On your feet!' snapped the Grey Lady.

As Lloyd struggled up, there was another thump, and Harvey landed beside him, trying not to cry. Lloyd gave him an encouraging nod, and he struggled to grin back, through his gag.

Thump! Thump! That was Ian and Mandy. The Grey Lady snapped out orders.

'Take them to Welcome Room Number Two and process them. Use Procedure Seventy-Three. It's almost time for HP9, and they must be kept out of the way until after that. *Those are Hunky's orders.*'

The men stood up very straight. '*Hunky's orders will be obeyed*,' they chanted.

There was something peculiar about the way they spoke, but Lloyd had no time to think about it. One of the men grabbed his arm and began to push him down the hill.

They were in a car-park, surrounded by a high brick wall. The ground sloped down towards the exit and, beyond that, Lloyd could see an assortment of strange roofs. The men hustled them through the gate and they found themselves facing a long, low building, with a huge sign over the door.

WELCOME TO MY STY
TROT IN AND PARK YOUR BACON!

The walls were splattered with brown stains and covered with grinning Hunky Parker faces, beaming in all directions. Lloyd shivered at the sight of them, but the men didn't take any notice. They pushed their prisoners through the door and into a big room with a large television screen and two rows of easy chairs.

Another Grey Lady was there to meet them. 'These are the snoopers, for Procedure Seventy-Three?'

The men nodded, and she waved a hand at the prisoners. 'Sit them down!'

One of the men knocked Lloyd backwards into a chair in the front row, facing the screen. Mandy, Harvey, and Ian were pushed down too, and the men slid into the chairs behind, ready to grab anyone who moved.

63

The Grey Lady picked up a remote control. 'Watch!' she ordered.

The screen flickered and grew bright, and Hunky Parker's horrible, smug voice filled the room. 'You made it! Now sit back and enjoy your first ED-u-cated holiday! Where even the weather does what you want.'

No! thought Lloyd. He wasn't going to watch another video with hidden pictures. Why should he let himself be tricked again? He closed his eyes.

The Grey Lady slapped the side of his face. 'Watch!'

Angrily, he opened his eyes again and glared at the screen. There was Hunky Parker, waddling towards a bright red door. The door opened —

— and Lloyd shrank back into his chair. Green eyes flamed out from behind the pig mask, staring straight at him. The ordinary, comic pig had disappeared, and they were watching the real Hunky Parker.

This time he didn't flash past. The camera moved into close-up, until the mask filled the screen, and the huge, luminous eyes stared out at them. And then the figure spoke.

'You have come a long way. You must be feeling tired and sleepy. Very, very sleepy . . .'

Lloyd felt as though he had been punched in the chest. *That* voice? Here? It was impossible!

'Look into my eyes,' the voice murmured. 'Look deep, deep into my eyes.'

Harvey was sitting bolt upright, and, next to him, Ian and Mandy were breathlessly still. They knew the voice too. Once upon a time, they had heard it every day, at school.

It was the Headmaster's voice.

And the eyes — Lloyd gazed at them. Why hadn't he recognized them before? Those cold, sea-green eyes that could take over almost anybody. Even Dinah hadn't had a chance against those eyes.

And now the Headmaster was Hunky Parker. And he was using the Welcome Suite to hypnotize everyone who came to The Sty!

Lloyd's mind moved like lightning. The Grey Lady mustn't guess that the four of them couldn't be hypnotized. If she did, they might be in desperate danger. They had to pretend.

Quickly, he leaned forward, fixing his eyes on the screen. Then, when he was sure the others were watching him, he let his eyelids droop, slowly and deliberately, as though the Headmaster's voice was sending him to sleep. There was no way of explaining. They *had* to understand!

Out of the corner of his eye, he saw Mandy's eyes widen in astonishment. For one, awful second, he thought she was going to give everything away. Then she realized what he was up to. Turning back to the screen, she let her eyelids droop too. So did Ian and Harvey.

Lloyd felt weak with relief. But there was no time to relax, because the soft, soothing voice from the screen suddenly changed.

'Open your eyes!' it snapped. 'Here are your instructions.'

65

* * *

For almost an hour, the voice talked steadily, filling their heads with complicated details that went on and on. . . . *Listen to this sound. At the first whistle, you will stand absolutely still. At the second one, you will follow the woman in grey overalls . . . You will do the work that is given to you . . . You will remember nothing of what happens outside the Dome . . . You will obey the women in grey overalls . . .*

None of it made any sense to Lloyd. Surely The Sty was a holiday place? What was all the talk about work? The video didn't give any explanation. Just orders and more orders.

Lloyd struggled to remember them all. He knew he had to obey them as though they were implanted in his brain, but by the end of the video his head was spinning.

There was no time to collect his thoughts. As the screen went fuzzy, the Grey Lady turned off the machine. Then she walked briskly up to him, hauled him to his feet and ripped off the gag.

'*Those are Hunky's orders,*' she said crisply.

For a split second, Lloyd fumbled for an answer. Then it came back to him, and he chanted it mechanically. '*Hunky's orders will be obeyed.*'

The Grey Lady nodded, satisfied, and waved to the men to untie him. Then she moved on to take off Mandy's gag.

'*Those are Hunky's orders.*'

Lloyd held his breath, but all the others had the right idea. Even Harvey. The answers snapped back, almost before the Grey Lady had finished speaking.

'*Hunky's orders will be obeyed.*'

When they were all untied, the Grey Lady nodded again and marched across the room to a door on the far side, away from the car-park.

'Take them straight to the Dome,' she snapped. 'They must be handed over before the weather changes.'

A hand was planted in the middle of Lloyd's back, propelling him towards the door. He stepped through, just behind Harvey — and gaped.

They were staring across a large, grassy space. On each side, the ground sloped down. To the left, it was covered with hundreds of brightly painted chalets and, to the right, a huge, ugly, grey building straggled down the hill. But Lloyd hardly glanced at any of that. Because, in the middle, looking back at him across the grass, was Hunky Parker's face.

But it was Hunky Parker blown up to a nightmare size. His chin rested on the ground, his ears were fifteen metres up in the air and his spiteful, piggy eyes gleamed like two enormous searchlights above a cavernous mouth.

And he was moving. The bristly ears twitched backwards and forwards, *left, right, left, right,* and black numbers flickered inside the nostrils.

Numbers that changed.

13:42

13:43

13:44

As he marched across the grass, Lloyd realized that he

was walking towards a gigantic clock. The ears ticked in time to the seconds, and the hours and minutes showed in the nostrils.

But that wasn't all. There were things moving in the mouth, as well. Things that looked like —

'People!' muttered Mandy, under her breath.

Lloyd nodded. The nightmare face wasn't just a clock. It was the front of a building, and its wide-open mouth was the doorway. Behind big glass doors, people in bright clothes were strolling about.

But it was a very weird building. Behind Hunky's face, glass walls curved up and away in a gigantic Dome that flashed in the midday sun. The inside of the Dome was full of something white and glittering.

Waiting by the door was yet another Grey Lady, with the same sharp expression as the others. But her overalls were thick and padded, like a ski suit, and she was wearing ski boots on her feet.

'Snow today,' she said crisply. She held out four bright blue ski suits and four knitted hats. 'Put these on!'

. . . *You will obey the women in grey overalls* . . . Quickly, Lloyd pulled on one set of clothes and sat down to tug on the boots. Ian was already lacing his up, and Mandy was helping Harvey to wriggle into his suit. In a few moments, all four of them were standing in line, waiting for instructions.

The Grey Lady pushed open one of the glass doors and pointed into the gaping pig-mouth. 'In you go!'

Side by side, trying not to shudder, they stepped over the threshold.

Instantly, they were hit by freezing cold air. Behind the pig-face, it was winter, and the Dome was full of snow. It crunched under their feet and fluttered in flakes from the ceiling, cushioning every ledge.

On one side, some children were building snowmen and having a snowball fight, and over the far side, against the back wall, was a hot dog stand, with a huge banner draped above it.

SUN TOMORROW, SNOW TODAY

But what dominated the whole Dome was the enormous slide in the middle, that swooped from ceiling to floor in a rippling cascade, carpeted with snow. The circular staircase that led to the summit was full of people with skis, climbing towards the shelter at the top.

When they reached it, they disappeared inside and put on their skis. They came zooming down the slide in a steady stream, one behind the other, like a mammoth, multi-coloured waterfall.

Lloyd frowned. It certainly looked like a holiday place. Why had all the Headmaster's instructions been about work?

The Grey Lady stood behind them, blocking the doorway. 'Enjoy yourselves. But don't meddle. *What does Hunky say?*'

69

Lloyd was so busy staring into the Dome that, for a moment, he didn't remember what he was meant to do. Suddenly, he realized that she was looking suspiciously at him.

What was he supposed to say?

'I . . . er —'

Desperately, he tugged at Ian's sleeve, hoping he could remember the right reply. But it was too late. The

Grey Lady's eyes hardened and she whirled round to call back the men in brown overalls.

'These four have not been properly processed!'

There was no time to lose. Immediately, the men turned and began to run towards them. Lloyd grabbed Harvey's sleeve and escaped in the only direction he could. He charged straight into the Dome, with Ian and Mandy right behind him.

71

There wasn't much hope of escaping, with the men so close, but Lloyd dragged Harvey into the middle of the nearest crowd and then looked over his shoulder for the others.

He couldn't see them.

The whole Dome was full of people in red and blue snowsuits, with woolly hats pulled down over their eyes. Through the fluttering snowflakes, everyone looked the same. Lloyd had to stand still and look very carefully to spot Ian and Mandy.

And if *he* couldn't spot them . . .

Perhaps they *could* escape! If they walked calmly through the crowd, they might be able to hide somewhere before the men found them.

Frantically, Lloyd looked round the Dome. He could see the men at the doorway now, looking round for them. And there were no corners to hide in, no little buildings to duck behind. Even the hot dog stand was right up against the back wall, and there was nothing else, except the ski slide.

The slide!

Lloyd leaned close to Harvey and whispered in his ear. 'Come on. Head for the slide.'

'But — ' Harvey swallowed, as Lloyd began heading towards the bottom of the spiral staircase. 'We'll break our legs.'

'We're not going to *ski*,' hissed Lloyd. He glanced over his shoulder, to make sure that Ian and Mandy were following. 'We're going to hide in the cabin at the top.'

72

Harvey frowned. 'For ever?'

'Of course not, you ding-brain!' Lloyd rolled his eyes. 'Just until this place shuts down for the night.'

'But — '

'Marigold marzipan, come *on*! If we hang around here, the men are sure to find us.'

Hauling Harvey after him, Lloyd ploughed through the snow, towards the gigantic slide.

Chapter 8

The Workshop

Dinah and Ingrid were battered black and blue as they travelled up the motorway. The big wooden crates slid around in the back of their lorry, crashing against them, and scratching them with rough corners and Ingrid moaned every time one hit her. But Dinah hardly noticed. She was desperately trying to remember everything she'd read about The Sty.

'It's a holiday place, isn't it, Ing? And there's something peculiar about the weather there.'

'Sun and snow together.' Ingrid frowned. 'There's even snow there in the summer. When I was in Wales, at Aunty Rachel's, the papers kept having competitions to win holidays there.'

'But why would they take Lloyd and the others somewhere like that?'

Ingrid shrugged. 'How should I know — OUCH! Stop going on about it. We'll find out soon enough.'

But it didn't seem soon. They were travelling for hours, first on the motorway and then on a narrow, twisting road. And, all the time, Ingrid grew crosser and crosser and Dinah got more worried.

Then, suddenly, they bumped over a hump in the road. Followed by another one. Dinah sat bolt upright.

'Ing! I think we're almost there!'

'So?' Ingrid yawned.

'We've got to hide.'

'Here?' snorted Ingrid. 'Oh, brilliant! Let's climb into the crates, shall we, and pretend to be bundles of baby clothes!'

It was meant as a joke, but Dinah didn't laugh. 'That's the only thing we *can* do,' she said firmly. 'And it might work. They're pretty strong crates, and they've got lids.'

She pushed Ingrid towards the nearest one and helped her climb in. Then she jammed the lid on top of her.

'I'd need a hammer to fix it properly, but it doesn't look too bad.'

'I'll probably suffocate,' Ingrid grumbled.

'The air'll last longer if you don't talk,' Dinah said. She was climbing into the next crate, and she wasn't going to waste time quarrelling. She needed to work out how to put a lid over herself, when she was already inside.

In the end, she found two nails sticking through the edges of the lid and held on to them. It wasn't very secure, but it was the best she could do.

There was no time to do anything different, because the lorry was backing into position, ready to stop. Dinah took a deep breath and braced herself, waiting for the doors to open.

But they didn't. She heard a clang as other doors were unfastened, but no one moved on to their lorry. Instead, there was a buzz of talk, too far away for her to make out

75

any words. Then several pairs of feet marched past them and out of earshot. And still no one came.

'I bet we'll be here for weeks!' grumbled Ingrid. 'For *years*. We'll starve to death, and when they open the crates they'll find our skeletons.'

'Sssh!' hissed Dinah. 'Or someone *will* come.'

'No, they won't,' Ingrid said crossly. 'I bet we're in the middle of . . . of a *forest*. Or half-way up a mountain, with not a house in sight. Or — '

'Sssh!'

'But I can't just huddle here. It's been *hours*. I — '

Ingrid stopped dead. Brisk footsteps were coming towards their lorry. One pair of high heels, with metal tips, and two pairs of flat shoes.

'Unload this one first,' said a woman's crisp voice. 'I'll go into my office and get the documents.'

Dinah and Ingrid were very still now. They hunched inside their boxes, hardly daring to breathe.

There was a rattle and a clang as the doors were unfastened and flung open. Suddenly it was much lighter in the boxes. Dinah could see the wooden sides, and the two bent nails that she was clutching. She gripped them firmly, and hoped.

The next moment, she was tipped sideways, as her box was lifted into the air.

'Thought all these crates were empty,' said a man's voice, grumbling. 'This one weighs a ton. What's it got inside?'

'Search me,' said the other man. 'Think we ought to take a look?'

Dinah froze. They were going to pull off the lid! They were going to drag her out of the box!

But the first man was hesitating. And when he replied, it was in a strange, singsong voice.

'What does Hunky say?'

The answer came back in exactly the same, mechanical singsong.

'Hunky says no snooping.'

A slow shiver went up Dinah's back. That was how the people at Parker Products had talked. And it reminded her of something . . . But it was impossible to think. Her whole body jarred as her box was flung down on to a trolley. Then it thudded again as another box was dumped on top.

'That one's heavy too,' said the grumbling voice. 'Think this is the right load?'

'We'll ask the Despatch Co-ordinator when we get them inside. Come on.'

The boxes tilted again as the trolley was tipped up, and the wheels rattled down a slope. There was a little crack in the wood, close by Dinah's eye, and she leaned forward to peer through it.

They were being wheeled down a long, narrow car-park, towards a gate at the far end. Ahead of them was a small building with garish paintings on the walls, and some words over the door

. . . COME TO MY S . . .
. . . T IN AND PARK YOUR B . . .

Before Dinah could make them out properly, the trolley swung right, round the building. She caught a brief glimpse of a high, glittering dome — glass? — and then found herself staring at a blank wall.

She was outside a building that looked like a vast factory. It was huge and grey, sprawling down the slope to the right, and its walls were perfectly plain. There was no window, and no nameplate to show what happened inside.

The trolley clattered through the nearest door, and Dinah saw a thin, upright figure marching towards them, carrying a clipboard. A Grey Lady, like the one at Parker Products.

'Over there!' she snapped.

'These crates aren't empty,' said the man who was pushing the trolley. 'Think we ought to look inside?'

The Grey Lady sighed impatiently, and rattled her nails on her clipboard. 'Where are the documents that go with them?'

'There aren't any documents.'

'Of *course* there are! If goods are being sent back, there'll be documents to tell us why. You must have left them in the lorry.'

'We didn't see any.'

The Grey Lady sighed again, even more impatiently, and tucked her clipboard under her arm. 'I suppose I shall have to find them myself. Come on!'

Her heels clicked on the concrete floor as she marched over to the door and the men followed her, muttering under their breath.

Dinah knocked on the lid of her crate. 'Ing!' she called, very softly. 'Is that you up there?'

'Thank goodness!' Ingrid called back. 'I didn't know what had happened to you.'

She sounded nervous, but Dinah had no time to reassure her. The Grey Lady wouldn't be gone for long. 'Can you see out? Is there anyone else around?'

There was a creak as Ingrid heaved off the top of her crate. Then she scrambled out, with a lurch, and lifted the crate off the trolley.

'Give me your lid, Di.'

'Thanks.' Gratefully, Dinah scrambled out. 'Put them back the way they were. Quickly. We've got to hide.'

For once, Ingrid didn't argue. She jammed the lid back on to the top crate and slid it into place while Dinah glanced round the store-room.

'Maybe we could hide behind one of those piles of boxes.'

'I've had enough of boxes,' Ingrid said firmly. 'What's behind that door? The one over there?'

She pointed to a door on the far side of the store. It stood slightly ajar and, through the glass panel in the top, Dinah could see the top of a filing cabinet.

'It must be the Grey Lady's office.'

'Let's go and see!'

Darting across the store-room, Ingrid disappeared

79

into the office. There was nothing Dinah could do except follow her. By the time she caught up, Ingrid was at the back of the office.

'Look, there's another door here.' She waved her hand at the glass panel. 'We can get out on this side.' She pressed down the handle as Dinah peered through at the narrow grey corridor beyond.

But the door was locked.

Ingrid scowled, but there was no time to do anything else. Already, they could hear the Grey Lady's spiky footsteps coming towards the store-room.

'Quick!' hissed Dinah. 'Duck down behind the filing cabinets!'

They crouched low, well out of sight of the store. Out there, the Grey Lady was shouting at the men.

'If there are no documents, the crates *must* be empty. Look!'

She flung the lids to the floor, with a clatter, and there was a dissatisfied mumble from the men. The Grey Lady didn't take any notice.

'You'd do better to get on with the job and mind your own business!' she snapped. '*What does Hunky say?*'

Behind the filing cabinets, Dinah held her breath. That question again! And the reply came back mechanically, just as she expected.

'*Hunky says no snooping.*'

'They're like *robots!*' hissed Ingrid. She shuddered.

Dinah nodded and let her eyes travel round the office. The most striking thing there was a large notice stuck on

80

the wall beside the desk. The months of the year were listed in big black letters, with words filled in beside them.

JANUARY FEBRUARY MARCH APRIL 1–13	HUNKY PARKER
APRIL 13	HP9
APRIL 14–30 MAY JUNE	APE! (CONTROLLED RIOTS)
JULY	TOTAL TAKEOVER

Controlled riots? Dinah had a sudden, sharp memory of the crowd marching down the hill, outside the bookshop. Was that a controlled riot?

If so—*who was controlling it?*

And were there going to be more of them?

The corner where she was crouching felt suddenly very chilly. If only they could get through that other door, and see where the grey corridor led! Maybe they would find out something then. If only the door hadn't been locked . . .

And then she saw the keys. A fat bunch of keys, hanging on a hook beside the desk. She nudged Ingrid.

'I'll go and try them,' she mouthed. 'Keep still.'

Very carefully, she inched across the floor, keeping one

ear on the Grey Lady's voice as she snapped out orders to the men in brown overalls. With her heart pounding, she stuck up a hand towards the hook.

No one saw her. A second later, she was huddled at the foot of the door, sorting through the keys. Not that one. Or that one. But maybe that, or that, or that . . .

It was the fifth key she tried. It turned smoothly in the lock, without a sound, and the door handle went down easily. Dinah wriggled back to the desk, to hang up the keys. Then she stuck her head up cautiously, to see what was going on in the store-room.

The Grey Lady was standing with her back to them, checking off the crates as the men brought them in. And the trolley rattled very loudly. The next time the men came in, Dinah touched Ingrid's elbow. 'Quick!' she mouthed.

They slithered across the floor, Dinah in front, and Ingrid a few feet behind. Dinah's heart pounded, but the rattle of the trolley covered the noise as the door opened. She crawled through it and down the corridor to the first corner. Wherever that corridor led, it couldn't be more dangerous than staying in the Grey Lady's office. She waited for Ingrid, and then stood up.

'Let's get going, shall we?'

Ingrid scrambled to her feet, looking smug. 'Look what I've got!'

She held out her hand. There, swinging from one finger, was the fat bunch of keys.

'You idiot!' Dinah gasped. 'If she sees they're missing,

she'll know someone's been in her office. Put them back!'

'Shan't,' said Ingrid. She stuck out her tongue at Dinah and ran past her, on tiptoe, towards the end of the corridor.

Dinah ran too. It was stupid to take risks like that. They had to put the keys back. She would *make* Ingrid . . .

But she didn't make Ingrid do anything, because she didn't catch up with her until the corner. And when they reached the corner, they saw something that made them both stop dead. Something that drove the keys right out of Dinah's mind.

Round the corner, the corridor was wider and one side of it was made up of big windows. But they were not windows to the outside. They looked into a huge room, crowded with brightly dressed people. There were men and women and children, some of them in swimsuits and some in shorts, or sundresses. All ready for the beach.

But they were nowhere near a beach. They were sitting in front of machines or bent over conveyor belts. Every single one — man, woman, or child — was working flat out.

And all their faces were completely blank and glazed.

Huge machines spewed out garish plastic toys. Sewing machines whizzed round the sides of fancy T-shirts and tracksuits. An enormous printing press was thudding away in the background, turning out heaps of luridly-coloured books. Everything in the room was bright and lively.

Except the people. There were hundreds of them

tending the machines, but no one smiled or spoke. They all stared straight down at what they were doing, almost without blinking.

Ingrid's mouth fell open. 'I thought we were at The Sty. But those people aren't on holiday.'

'They're dressed as if they were,' Dinah said grimly. 'There's something very odd going on, Ing. It's much too cold for beach clothes. Do you think — ?'

She didn't finish what she was saying. At that moment, a loud, shrill noise split the air. A whistle blast, amplified to a deafening level.

Immediately, all the people in the workshop stopped what they were doing and stepped back from the machines. They stood motionless, as though they were waiting for something to happen, and all their faces were completely blank.

The Grey Lady marched up and down between the machines, looking from side to side. *Click click click*. Her sharp metal heels seemed to measure the seconds as the big black hand swept round the clock face.

Then the whistle sounded again. Immediately, the frozen figures began to move. One behind the other, marching in step, they filed out of a door at the far end, walking like robots, with blank faces.

In a few seconds, the workshop was empty, except for the Grey Lady.

Chapter 9

Sun Tomorrow?

Lloyd could see the men in brown overalls fanning out across the Dome, like hounds searching for a scent. He longed to race to the ski slide, but he knew they would be spotted if he did. He had to plod along slowly, like the other holidaymakers.

By the time he and Harvey reached the bottom of the circular staircase, the men were zigzagging methodically from one side of the Dome to the other. Lloyd forced himself to stop at the ski stall, at the bottom of the stairs, and wait while the man in charge found him a pair of skis. Then, at last, he began to climb.

Once he was above the heads of the crowd, he could see the whole, snow-filled Dome. It was easy to spot the men who were following them. They looked cold and shivering, but they didn't stop searching for a moment. Right and left, behind and in front. From side to side and all around.

But not up.

Lloyd crossed his fingers and went on climbing. By the time he hauled himself up into the cabin at the top of the staircase, his arms ached and he was out of breath, but the men still hadn't spotted them.

There were several people in the cabin, putting on skis, but no one hung around. The moment the skis were on, the skiers stepped on to the slide and disappeared, in a flurry of snow. Followed by the next people. And the next, and the next.

When Ian and Mandy arrived, they huddled into a corner of the cabin beside Lloyd and Harvey, but no one else stopped long enough to notice them. The skiers passed through at top speed, cascading over the top and down the slide.

Lloyd took a look through the slatted side of the cabin. Then he beckoned to the others to lean close.

'We've got to *think*.'

'Are you sure there's time?' murmured Ian. 'I don't want to worry you, but look down there.'

Lloyd glanced down. The staircase was almost empty. Three or four people were still climbing, but below them there was nobody. The man who had been handing out skis stood at the bottom with an arm out, closing the staircase off.

'He's found us,' Harvey said miserably. 'He's going to come up and get us.'

But the man didn't move. He just stood there, looking at his watch from time to time and shaking his head at people who tried to get past him.

The last skier stepped into the cabin, fastened his skis and disappeared down the slide. When he reached the bottom, a loud whistle echoed across the snow.

And everything stopped.

Every person in the Dome stood absolutely still. Even the children were motionless, with snowballs in their hands. No one made a sound, and nothing moved except a snowball that was thrown just as the whistle sounded. It flew across the Dome and hit a red-faced man square on the nose, but he didn't even blink. He went on staring straight ahead, as though nothing had happened.

Then there was a loud grating, creaking noise. Mandy gasped and pointed at the far wall of the Dome.

The whole thing was swivelling, including the hot dog stand and the SUN TOMORROW, SNOW TODAY banner. It turned in its place like a revolving door, rotating until it stuck straight out into the Dome. On either side of it yawned an enormous dark gap, leading into the space behind.

There was another blast on the whistle. Perfectly together, moving like machines, all the people in the Dome began to walk towards the gaps, forming neat, well-spaced lines and marching exactly in step. Only the men in brown overalls stood still, left on their own. Dark splodges on the whiteness of the snow.

As the last person disappeared behind the far wall, a door opened in the side of the Dome, and there was the guttural sound of an engine. In came a huge snowplough driven by a man in brown overalls. Briskly, it began to move round the Dome, pushing the snow towards the back wall and through the gaps.

When the ground was almost clear, there was a loud click, and then a whirring sound. Suddenly, a gust of wind hit the cabin on the top of the slide, whistling between the slats. Looking round, Lloyd saw two giant fans whirring on the wall, above the front door of the Dome.

He couldn't see them for long. By the time they got up to full speed, the air was full of flying snow. The wind caught it and whirled it up into the air, blowing it off all the ledges, across the Dome and out into the black space at the back.

'I'm c-cold!' stuttered Harvey, his teeth chattering. The snow was blowing into the shelter, catching on his face and stinging his cheeks.

'Quick!' Mandy put one arm round him and one round Ian, pulling them towards her. 'Huddle together, before we freeze!'

The four of them formed a tight knot, with their backs to the flying snow, and the wind roared on and on, whipping round the backs of their necks and nipping their fingers. They were so busy sheltering from it that they didn't have time to think about anything else.

Until they began to get hot.

Quite suddenly, they found themselves gasping and panting for air, and Harvey pulled away from the huddle.

'I can't . . . breathe!' he panted. 'I'm boiling!'

Lloyd stepped back too, loosening the neck of his ski suit. 'You're right! Scarlet sausages, it's like an oven in here!'

He leaned over to look between the slats — and gasped. 'It's *changed*. It's changed completely!'

* * *

All the snow had vanished. The Dome was full of green plants, arching high above the ground and spreading long, lush tendrils over trellised screens. The floor, which had been covered by nearly a metre of snow, was paved, and patched with grass, and there were sunloungers everywhere, and little tables with umbrellas.

'It's like being *abroad*!' breathed Harvey. 'It's like the *beach*!'

'Fancy a swim, do you?' drawled Ian.

He pointed down the slide. It wasn't a ski slide any more. Now, it swooped towards a shimmering blue swimming pool, with water plants round the edges and a little island in the middle.

'What a wonderful water-chute!' whispered Mandy.

Ian frowned. 'The problem with water-chutes is —'

He didn't have time to say what the problem was. Suddenly, there was a hiss from the far side of the shelter. A jet of water shot out of the wall and hit all four of them.

They went flying forwards, knocked off their feet. Harvey skidded in the water, fell over and slipped down the ramp with a squeal. Lloyd slid after him. And behind them, tumbling awkwardly from side to side of the chute, came Ian and Mandy, heading straight for the water.

Lloyd hit it with a huge splash, almost on top of Harvey. For a few seconds his ski suit buoyed him up, and he grabbed at Harvey's shoulder as Ian and Mandy splashed down behind them.

'Got to . . . swim to the side!' he panted. 'Before . . . our clothes get heavy.'

90

But Harvey was treading water and staring across the Dome. 'Look!'

Was it the men in brown overalls? Lloyd flipped round — and gasped again.

The men were watching them all right, but they couldn't get near the pool because of the stream of people in between. Hundreds of men, women, and children, in swimming costumes and shorts, were marching out of the dark space at the end, where the skiers had disappeared. They moved quickly, but their faces were completely blank, and they weren't laughing or talking to each other. They simply walked into the Dome, found a space to stand, and stopped.

When the last person had walked in, the grating, creaking noise started up again. The end wall of the Dome began to turn, just as it had before, until its other side was facing inwards. Where the hot dog stall had been, there was a bar selling drinks and icecream and, draped above it, was a banner which said

SNOW TOMORROW, SUN TODAY!

As soon as the wall was in place, the shrill whistle sounded, and immediately, all the people woke up. They began laughing and chatting, as though they had been in the Dome for a long time. Some of them plunged into the pool, but a lot more headed for the circular staircase and began climbing up towards the water chute.

The men in brown overalls moved too. As soon as the

whistle blew, they began to pick their way through the crowd, not running, but heading straight for the swimming pool.

'Hurry!' hissed Mandy. 'We've got to get out of here!'

She swam across the pool, to the side furthest away from the men, and began to haul herself out. A little boy pointed at her and giggled.

'Look, Mummy, they've got it wrong! They think it's skiing today!' He went off into peals of laughter, saying the words over and over again. 'They think it's skiing! They think it's skiing!'

Lloyd reached the side and pulled himself out of the water. 'It *was* skiing an hour ago,' he said loudly.

The little boy's mother smiled. 'It's muddling sometimes, isn't it? But it's been sun all day today. I've been sunbathing since breakfast.' She waved her hand towards a sunlounger at the side of the pool.

'You haven't!' Lloyd said. 'You've only just come!'

The woman's smile disappeared. 'Don't be silly, dear. I know what I've been doing.'

'But —'

Ian stuck his head between them. 'It's no use, Lloyd. She won't believe you, and you haven't got time to argue. Look.'

Lloyd glanced round. Half a dozen men in brown overalls were closing in on them. They were spread out in a half circle, blocking the main door and both the fire exits.

There was only one way to run. Towards the end wall,

92

where the big banner hung over the bar. Lloyd couldn't see a door there, but there had to be a way through. That was where the skiers had gone.

'Come on!' he hissed at the others. 'Follow me!'

One or two people turned to stare as they pushed through the crowd, and a couple of children giggled, but most people were too busy to take any notice. They were buying H.P.'s Ice Cream Soda (Stick Your Snout in One of These!) or pumping up their Sty-los, ready to float in the pool. They weren't interested in four children in dripping wet ski suits.

Or in the men who were following them. The men in brown overalls slipped through the crowd without drawing attention to themselves. Closing in, steadily and relentlessly.

Harvey looked despairingly at the end wall. 'There isn't a door, L! What are we going to do?'

'Vermilion vermicelli, how should I know?' Lloyd gazed at the wall. It was covered with thick creepers, and it didn't look as though it had ever moved at all.

'We'll have to dodge back,' Mandy said faintly. 'Maybe if we split up — '

But she didn't bother to finish. They could all see that was no good. There was no way of getting past the men. They were being slowly herded towards the wall, and when they reached it, they would be caught.

'Get ready to make a lot of noise,' murmured Ian. 'If we're dragged off yelling, people *might* wonder what's happening. Ready?'

93

But Lloyd was still staring at the wall. 'Hang on!' he hissed. 'Look at that!'

Hidden among the creepers was a long, iron ladder. It led right up to the top of the Dome, to a trapdoor in the roof. Lloyd grabbed the sides with both hands and began to haul himself up.

Harvey scrambled on behind, so close that his hands brushed Lloyd's ankles, and Ian followed. But Mandy darted away from the ladder, towards the nearest sun-lounger.

'No!' Lloyd called. 'They'll catch you!'

Mandy grinned over her shoulder. Then she bent to pick something up from the sunlounger, pushing it into her trouser pocket. When she leapt for the ladder, the men were only ten metres behind.

'Quick!' she panted. 'Get as high as you can, Lloyd. I'm going to stop them following us!'

By the time the men reached the bottom of the ladder, Mandy was high above their heads. She stopped, and pulled a blue plastic bottle out of her pocket. As she unscrewed the cap, Lloyd peered down at the words on the bottle.

HUNKY'S SPECIAL SUNTAN OIL
THE WAY TO BROWN YOUR BACON!

Clinging on with one hand, Mandy bent down and tipped the suntan oil down the ladder, just as the first man began to climb. As it dripped greasily from rung to rung, Mandy began to climb again, watching over her shoulder.

One man was on the ladder. He managed another two or three rungs, but then his hands began to slip on the oil.

'You little — !!!' he yelled.

He went slithering backwards, trailing oil all the way down to the bottom and landing on top of the other men.

'Climb!' yelled Lloyd. 'They can't follow us!'

Harvey gave a little squeak. 'It's very high.'

'Don't look. Just keep climbing.'

Harvey scrambled higher, and Lloyd kept ahead of him, gazing up at the trapdoor in the roof. He thought it would be locked, but when he reached the top of the ladder and pushed, it flicked open easily.

Fresh, cool air flooded down. Lloyd pulled himself through on to the roof and lay there panting, looking down through the arching glass.

Men in brown overalls were racing towards the Dome from every side, fanning out to surround it. As Harvey came through the trapdoor he saw them too, and his bottom lip trembled.

'We'll never be able to get down. They're all over the grass.'

But Lloyd was looking the other way, towards the ugly building attached to the back of the Dome. 'We could get down on to that roof. Look.'

The building was a dull grey box, over a hundred metres long. It looked more like a warehouse or a factory than part of a holiday centre. There were no words painted on it. No pictures of Hunky Parker. Not a single speck of colour to brighten it up.

Except for the squares of blue, where the sky was reflected in the skylights.

Lloyd stared at those skylights — and suddenly he knew what they had to do. 'We can't get down, but we can try getting *in*. I bet there are lots of hiding places in that building.'

Ian nodded as he climbed through the trapdoor. 'If we keep low, the men won't be able to see where we go.'

Dropping on to his front, Lloyd wriggled towards the flat roof. By the time Mandy scrambled out of the Dome, he was already ten metres away, examining the first skylight.

'This one's locked. But there's some kind of workshop down there. With lots of machines and things. No one's working, but — whoops!' He jerked his head back quickly as a Grey Lady walked underneath.

'Be careful!' hissed Mandy.

Ian waved his hand at the next skylight. 'How about that? It looks half open.'

Lloyd wriggled a bit further and peered in. 'It looks like a television studio. There are cameras and scenery screens, and big lights on stands. And a control room — '

'Never mind what it's for,' muttered Ian. 'Is there anyone in there?'

Lloyd checked carefully. 'No one at all. And there are two doors at the other end. Both open.'

'Let's get down there, then!'

'Here I go!' Lloyd let himself down as far as he could and dropped the rest of the way. Then he glanced round.

He was at one end of a large studio, with nothing around him except bare, polished floor. The cameras and scenery screens were half-way down and at the far end was a control room with glass sides, built along the wall between the two doors.

The only strange thing was a groove in the floor. It ran from one side of the studio to the other, in between where he was standing and everything else. For a second, Lloyd stared down at it. Then two feet kicked him in the back.

'Catch me, L!'

97

Harvey slithered into his arms, and Ian and Mandy followed.

'Right!' hissed Lloyd, as Mandy hit the floor. 'Let's get going!'

He took one step towards the doors.

Immediately, there was a loud rattle from in front of him. Before he could move any further, a thick metal grille rose out of the groove in the floor.

At the same moment, with a harsh, grating noise, a metal plate slid across the skylight opening, blocking it off completely.

They were caged in!

Chapter 10

APE!

Dinah and Ingrid were trapped. They stared into the empty workshop, listening to the *click click click* of the Grey Lady's heels as she walked up and down between the machines. Watching.

Ingrid scowled. 'Why doesn't she go away?'

'I think she's waiting for something,' Dinah said slowly. 'She keeps looking up at the clock.'

Click click.

Suddenly, the Grey Lady stopped. She glanced at the clock again, then walked across to the door at the end of the workshop and flung it open.

In marched another long line of people. They were just like the people who had left. Blank-faced and mechanical. But they weren't dressed for the beach. They were wearing thick padded suits in bright colours, and most of them had woolly hats on their heads.

'They look like *skiers*,' muttered Ingrid.

Dinah nodded. 'They must be sweltering.'

If they were, they didn't show it. They moved where the Grey Lady pointed, going to the machines that the beach people had just left. When they reached their places, they stood motionless and silent, until the whistle sounded again.

Then, immediately, every machine in the workshop

whirred into action, and the skiers bent forward to begin their tasks, working like lightning.

Ingrid shuddered. '*They* make the Hunky Parker things?'

'Suppose so.' Dinah leaned forward, looking for Hunky Parker's face, but she couldn't make it out. There was something on the things churned out of the machine — some kind of symbol — but it didn't seem quite right.

Ingrid snorted. 'I'm not hanging round to watch, even if you are.'

Before Dinah could grab her, she leapt out of the corner and went racing down the corridor, in full view of the workshop.

'Ing!'

It was sheer good luck that the Grey Lady didn't see anything. She had just stepped behind a big printing press that hid her completely. Before she emerged, Ingrid had reached the first door on the right. She pressed the handle, but it was locked. Whipping out the bunch of keys, she began to try them, one by one.

'Come back!' Dinah was sure the Grey Lady would see. Any minute now, she would be coming out from behind the printing press.

But, just in time, Ingrid found the right key. Unlocking the door, she disappeared through it with a triumphant grin — leaving Dinah trapped in the corner as the Grey Lady turned to stare through the window.

She seemed to stare for ever, but at last she began to

march round the workshop again, inspecting everything with her sharp, bright eyes. Dinah held her breath, waiting. Then, the moment the Grey Lady reached the printing press again, she dashed. She scuttled ten metres down the corridor and darted in at the door where Ingrid had disappeared.

'Ing?'

But the room was empty.

There were charts and graphs all over the walls, and a big table in the middle, with nine or ten chairs round it, but Ingrid wasn't there. There was nothing else in the room, except a tall cupboard on the right hand side.

'Where are you?' Dinah called softly.

There was a deep grunt from inside the cupboard.

'Stop fooling about!'

There was another grunt. The cupboard creaked. Then it flew open and a massive figure lurched out. Six feet tall, with a huge, hairy head and enormous, clutching hands that reached out to grab Dinah.

A giant ape.

'What — ?' For a second, Dinah was rigid with terror. Then the ape lurched towards her and she dodged sideways, just in time.

The ape turned to follow and one of its legs wobbled and gave way.

'Whoops!' said a familiar voice.

'Ing!' Dinah grabbed furiously at the fur, and there was a giggle from behind the ferocious mask.

'Isn't it *brilliant*? There are things to stand on, inside the feet, a bit like being on stilts. You feel *gigantic*. What d'you think it's for?'

'I . . . I don't know.' Dinah studied the coarse, thick hair of the ape suit. 'Where did you find it?'

'It was locked in the cupboard.' Ingrid held up the keys, letting them swing from the metal label that said *Despatch Co-ordinator*. 'I undid the door and — AAARGH!' She staggered backwards, dramatically, and landed with her head against the wall.

Right beside a chart that looked very familiar to Dinah.

JANUARY		
FEBRUARY	}	HUNKY PARKER
MARCH		
APRIL 1–13		

APRIL 13 — HP9

APRIL 14–30			(CONTROLLED
MAY	}	APE!	RIOTS)
JUNE			

JULY — TOTAL TAKEOVER

APE! Dinah took a deep breath and pointed at the chart. 'Look, Ing. *That's* who you're dressed up as.'

Ingrid frowned. 'What does it mean?'

'I think . . . there's going to be a swap,' Dinah said slowly. 'After April the thirteenth, APE! will be the new craze, like Hunky Parker is now.'

'You mean we're going to be wearing hairy tracksuits? And trainers with five fingers where the toes ought to be?'

'Something like that,' said Dinah. 'Maybe — '

Click click click.

'What's that?' muttered Ingrid. *Click click click*. There were footsteps outside. Someone was coming down the corridor, towards them.

103

'Quick!' Seizing Ingrid's shoulder, Dinah dragged her into the cupboard and pulled the door shut. 'Keep still!' she hissed. 'Don't make a sound!'

Ingrid opened her mouth to argue — and then shut it again. The feet had stopped outside their door. It opened and someone marched in, walking briskly up to the table and pulling out a chair to sit on. Dinah held her breath.

A second later, there were more footsteps. *Click click click*. And then more, and more, until seven people had walked in altogether. Dinah couldn't bear it. She *had* to see what was going on. Very, very carefully, she opened the door a crack.

Seven Grey Ladies were sitting round the table with briefcases by their sides and neat clipboards in front of them. All of them were dressed in identical grey overalls, with their hair pulled back into tight little buns, and all of them were rigidly upright, staring towards the door as though they were waiting for someone else to appear.

It was a few seconds before the last person came down the corridor, and this time the footsteps were quite different. Quieter and heavier. When they reached the door, the Grey Ladies glanced at each other and got up, standing stiffly to attention. Dinah clenched her fists nervously.

The door opened. All together, the Grey Ladies chorused, 'Good morning, Hunky.'

There was no answering greeting. A tall figure marched up to the far end of the table and pulled out a chair. Then it turned —

— and Dinah found herself gazing at the face from the video. Hunky Parker himself, with his stiff, unchanging mask and his terrible eyes. She clenched her fists harder, until the fingernails dug into her skin.

Then the figure spoke. 'Let us begin, without wasting any more time.'

For a second, Dinah couldn't hear anything else. Her head spun, and the blood pounded in her ears. The last time she had heard *that voice*, it had been plotting to take over the Prime Minister's brain. And she had nearly burnt to death trying to stop the plot. Her heart began to thud, but she forced herself to go on looking.

The heavy mask covered the figure's head completely. It was perfectly modelled, with every disgusting detail bright and clear. The nostrils were slimy, the ears were spattered with mud, and there was a trail of saliva at the corner of the mouth. But the voice coming out of the mouth was unmistakable. It belonged to the Headmaster — who couldn't bear mess and disorder.

'So far, my plans have gone smoothly,' snapped the voice. 'All the shops in the country are full of Hunky Parker goods, and when people cannot get them, they riot. Exactly as I intended.'

Dinah remembered the crowd on the hill, and shuddered.

'Those riots will spread all over the country,' the voice went on, 'when HP9 goes out. People will want APE! instead of Hunky Parker — but there will be nothing for them to buy. So they will smash, and loot, and run wild.'

105

Dinah held her breath, and Ingrid stood stock still. They both knew they mustn't get caught. They *had* to find out what was going on.

'I shall allow the riots to continue for approximately ten weeks,' said the Headmaster. 'I expect several deaths in that time, and considerable destruction of property.'

Why? thought Dinah. She could hardly believe her ears. Why should the Headmaster want that?

He obviously wasn't going to explain. Instead, he looked briskly up and down the table. 'Is everything prepared, as I instructed?'

One of the Grey Ladies rustled her papers efficiently. 'Preparations are on target. Everything will be ready when HP9 goes out, on the thirteenth of April.'

'That date has had to be changed!' snapped the Headmaster. 'Some meddling person has discovered the subliminal frames on a Hunky Parker video.'

The Grey Ladies gasped and, inside the cupboard, Dinah and Ingrid looked at each other.

But the green eyes behind the mask did not waver. 'Luckily,' said the Headmaster, 'we were warned in time. We have — retrieved that video. And all the unsold copies. But we must not take chances. So HP9 will not go out on the thirteenth of April. It will go out — today.'

There was a rustle, and another gasp.

The Headmaster ignored them. 'Because of this change of plan, the workshops will need to double their production. Please make sure that all the workers operate twice as fast as before. They must — '

A loud bleep interrupted him. There was a shocked mutter from the Grey Ladies and Dinah saw the Headmaster's eyes flicker as he pulled a telephone out of his pocket.

'Who is it?' he snapped.

A voice came crackling from the phone, loud enough for everyone to hear. 'There has been a failure of Procedure Seventy-Three. Snoopers have escaped into The Sty.'

'Procedure Seventy-Three *never* fails,' said one of the Grey Ladies sharply.

'Not if it is properly carried out,' said another.

The Headmaster silenced them with a look, and spoke into the phone. 'Where are the snoopers now?'

For one, terrible moment, Dinah thought the voice would say, *In the cupboard next to you,* but it didn't. The answer crackled back briskly.

'We have applied Procedure Seventeen, and the snoopers are trapped at the collection point.'

The Headmaster nodded. 'Excellent. I shall go and deal with them.' He put the phone away and looked round the table at the Grey Ladies. 'Go back and double the speed of the workshops, ready for HP9. And send a detachment of Manual Operatives to the collection point. Equipped with ropes.'

One of the Grey Ladies nodded. 'I will send them at once.'

The Headmaster stood up and led the way to the door. When he reached it, he turned and fixed all the Grey

Ladies with his chilly green stare. '*Those are Hunky's orders.*'

'*Hunky's orders will be obeyed*,' the Grey Ladies chanted together.

They stepped into the corridor and went clicking off to the left as the Headmaster turned right.

The moment they were gone, Ingrid burst out of the cupboard, waving her hairy arms furiously. 'Come on! We've got to follow! It must be Lloyd and the others they've got trapped.'

Dinah swallowed. 'But . . . we mustn't get caught. We might be the only people who know about this HP9 thing. Whatever it is. We've got to find a way of stopping the Headmaster.'

Ingrid looked impatient. 'We can deal with that when we've saved the others.'

She wrenched open the door — and then dived back into the room. There were a dozen men in brown overalls coming down the corridor towards them.

But it was too late to escape. The men had seen her and they headed straight for the door, tugging it open while her hand was still on the handle. One of them marched in and grabbed her shoulder. 'What's the fancy dress for?'

Another seized Dinah. 'What are you up to?'

They were enormous. They crowded into the doorway, completely blocking it, so that they hid the workshop on the other side of the corridor.

Ingrid's big APE!-mouth opened, but no words came out. Only a little, strangled squeak. Dinah didn't even try to speak.

'Come on.' The man who was holding Ingrid shook her shoulder fiercely. 'Are you snooping?'

'I . . . I — ' Ingrid's eyes stared desperately from behind the eyeholes of the mask, and Dinah struggled to think.

It was no use trying to run away. Even if they could get free, the men would catch them before they had gone ten metres. And the Grey Lady in the workshop would see them. But what *could* they do?

The men were glancing at each other. 'Procedure Ninety-Two?' said one.

'Ninety-*Four*,' said another. 'We have to fetch the Security Co-ordinator.'

No! Dinah felt frantic. That mustn't happen. If only she could think! She glanced round, wildly, and saw what the men were carrying. Ropes. They were equipped with ropes. *They were the Manual Operatives the Headmaster had asked for!*

Her brain went into hyper-drive. Pulling herself up straight, she glared at the men. 'We are going to come with you,' she said firmly. 'You are to let us come, but you must ignore us. You must not even look at us. *Those* — '

She could hardly believe it would work, but she had to try.

' — *those are Hunky's orders.*'

It was like magic. Immediately, the men who were holding on to them let go. All the men took a step backwards, and their eyes glazed over.

'*Hunky's orders will be obeyed,*' they chanted together. Then they turned to the right, ready to march down the corridor.

Dinah grabbed Ingrid's arm. 'Come on!'

'But — ' Ingrid hadn't understood.

'Don't you *see?*' Dinah said impatiently. 'They're going to where the others are. We can go with them — and they'll hide us!'

'Oh yes!'

Ingrid almost leapt through the door, tugging Dinah after her. As the men started to march, the two of them were close beside, completely hidden from the workshop by the huge, brown-overalled bodies.

Down one corridor they went, round a corner and along another corridor with dull grey walls on both sides. Dinah and Ingrid slipped to the back of the group, keeping a wary eye on where they were going.

They swung round into another corridor, and there was a closed door ahead of them. Above it was a red light, and the words Studio — Do Not Enter. And standing in front of the door was — the Headmaster.

Dinah's heart gave one, enormous thud. She grabbed Ingrid, and pulled her back round the corner. The two of them stood very, very still, listening hard. They heard

110

the door open. Then the Headmaster's voice spoke briskly, giving orders.

'Go straight into the studio, line up in front of the cage, and wait for me.'

The men moved in, at a steady tramp. Holding her breath, Dinah peered round the corner. She couldn't see much of the room, but just inside the door was a small glass booth packed with monitor screens and computer consoles. It looked like a control room. That might be a good place to hide, to watch what was going on in the studio. But did they dare try and get there?

She had just decided it was too risky when the Headmaster followed the men into the studio and closed the door.

Immediately, Ingrid darted round the corner, padding on her big, soft feet. 'Come on! We might be able to get into that little room thing!'

'But he'll see us!' protested Dinah.

'We've got to try! Come on!'

Before Dinah could say any more, Ingrid was at the door, pressing the handle down, slowly and softly. She peered into the room, and then glanced over her shoulder with a grin. Dropping on to her stomach, she began to wriggle towards the control room.

There was nothing Dinah could do. Except follow.

Chapter 11

Parcelled up!

Lloyd stood holding the bars of the cage and stared out into the studio. For a second, he had hoped there was a chance of escaping. But now he knew that it was no use. A line of men in brown overalls was marching into the room.

They were caught.

The men lined up in front of the cage, without speaking, staring straight ahead. Harvey blinked at them.

'D'you think we should try and explain?' he faltered.

'They don't look as though they've come for a chat,' muttered Ian.

'But they *are* people,' Mandy said bravely. 'Maybe — ' Nervously, she smiled at them through the bars.

Then her smile vanished, as someone else walked through the door. The line of brown-overalled men parted and between them walked a tall, thin figure in a mask.

Hunky Parker.

Harvey gave a little cry and stepped closer to Lloyd, and Mandy clenched her fists. They had all gone white and very still.

It was impossible to see what the person in the mask was thinking. But, when he spoke, his voice was like steel.

'So. You are interfering again. Where are the rest of you?'

'They got left behind,' Harvey said. His voice was trembling, but he sounded defiant. 'But they won't let you get away with this! They'll come after us!'

The Headmaster's eyes snapped. 'They will be too late! In a few hours, you will have vanished for ever. Unless you agree to — co-operate.'

'Co-operate? With you?' Lloyd snorted scornfully. '*We* won't be turned into holiday robots.'

Mandy slipped her arm round Harvey's shoulders and stared at the Headmaster. 'Why do you need to hypnotize those people anyway? They could have fun on their own, without that.'

'Fun?' There was a scornful snort from behind the Hunky Parker mask. 'You think the Dome was built for *fun*? So that people could waste their time and energy?'

'It looked like pretty good fun to me,' drawled Ian. 'Skiing down the snow slide. There's nothing useful about that.'

'On the contrary,' the Headmaster said scornfully. 'The Sty was specially designed to *use* all the energy people waste on slides. Everyone who goes down *my* slides is helping to drive the generator that powers this building.'

'You mean — they're producing *electricity* when they slide?' Lloyd stared. 'What for?'

'I can see that you have no idea what is going on here,' the Headmaster said smoothly. 'And I have no intention

113

of telling you. Twice already you have stood in my way. This time, I shall succeed. Today I am launching the plan that will put me in control of the country. But first — I shall get rid of you four.' He turned to the men in brown overalls. '*What do you see?*'

They replied together, their eyes glazing over as they chanted the words. '*We see what Hunky tells us.*'

'That is correct.' The Headmaster pointed towards the cage. 'What you see in this cage are four rolls of carpet, ready for despatch abroad. What you see?'

'Four rolls of carpet,' said the men obediently.

'Rubbish!' yelled Lloyd. 'Do I look like a roll of carpet? Watch!' He began to jump about, waving his arms and pulling faces at the men. 'Come on, you three. Show them!'

Harvey, Ian, and Mandy began to jump too, twisting their bodies around and yelling. But it was no use. The men didn't even blink, and the Headmaster went on giving orders.

'You are to take these carpets and bind them tightly with cords, from top to bottom.' A small smile crossed his face. 'So that they travel safely.'

Lloyd glared through the bars. 'It's no good. You won't get rid of us like that. If you send us away, we'll just come back!'

'You will?' The Headmaster sounded amused. 'I don't think so.' He turned to the men in brown overalls. 'Lower the bars and tie up the carpets.'

One of the men pulled down a lever in the wall and slowly, with a harsh grinding noise, the heavy bars began to sink back into the groove in the floor. There was no chance of escaping. The moment the bars were low enough, Lloyd was seized by three of the men in brown overalls. The others grabbed Harvey, Ian, and Mandy, and began to bind them tightly.

Their feet were tied together first. Then the men spun them round and round, wrapping them in cord from head to foot. For as long as he could, Lloyd shouted, trying to get the men to listen to him.

'Exploding emerald eggshells! Can't you see he's got you hypnotized? We're not carpets — we're children!'

It was no use. The men's expressions did not change at all.

Harvey's face grew pinker and pinker as he spun round. 'Where are we going, L? What's going to happen to us?'

'Don't be afraid,' Lloyd sounded as confident as he could. 'Wherever we're going, we can still stick together. We're SPLAT and — ugggh — '

The cord had reached his mouth. It slid in, gagging him, and he almost choked. But he could still see, and he shuddered at the Headmaster's smile.

The last knot was tied, and the men in brown overalls turned towards the Headmaster. 'The carpets are ready, sir. What shall we do with them?'

'Take them to Despatch,' said the Headmaster. 'They

must be parcelled up straight away, but they are not urgent. Tell the Despatch Co-ordinator they can be sent by sea.'

'Where are they to go?'

For a moment the Headmaster paused. Then he took out a pad of paper and began to write addresses, in neat black script.

'This one,' he pointed at Harvey, 'is to go to Burkina Faso. The tall one next to it — ' that was Ian ' — is for Sarawak.'

Different places! Lloyd hadn't thought of that. His heart sank as he struggled to remember the names of the places. The Headmaster moved along the line and prodded the bundle that was Mandy.

'This one is for Surinam.'

Where on earth was Surinam? Lloyd wished he had learned more geography. He could see enough of Mandy's face to guess that she knew where it was — and it wasn't anywhere near Wales.

'And this one — ' The Headmaster stopped for a moment when he got to Lloyd. He looked him up and down, frowning. 'This one had better go to Pitcairn Island.'

Pitcairn Island? Lloyd had never heard of it. But it sounded a long way away. He began to grunt and struggle, but the Headmaster ignored the noise. Stepping back, he waved a hand at the bundles.

'Obey your orders!'

Immediately, the men hoisted the four bundles on to

their shoulders. Lloyd found himself travelling head first, on his side, gazing at the wall. Beside him was Mandy, but he couldn't talk to her. And he couldn't turn and look at Harvey, who was grunting uncomfortably somewhere behind.

As they were carried off along the corridor, Lloyd struggled to wriggle his head round, just an inch or two, to get a glimpse of Harvey. But it was impossible. He was trussed too tight to move.

And then they went round a corner and he saw

117

something that drove everything else out of his head.

The corridor had a glass wall, and behind it was what looked like a factory running at top speed. At double top speed. The machines were rattling and thudding and the workers' hands were flying backwards and forwards, almost too fast to see.

That was peculiar enough, but there was something even odder. *Why were all the workers wearing skiing clothes?*

For a second, Lloyd was utterly bewildered. Then he saw a face he recognized. It was one of the children who'd been making a snowman in the Dome.

So *this* was where they'd disappeared to!

They'd come into the factory to work — and the people in beach clothes had gone out to have fun. And generate electricity.

Suddenly, it all started to make sense. People who came to The Sty thought they were going on holiday. But they were hypnotized as soon as they walked in, and after that they spent half their time working on machines — and the other half sliding down ramps to make the power that ran the machines.

And no one gave them any wages. They *paid* to be there. It was a wonderful scheme for making money.

For a second, even though he was trussed up and on his way to Pitcairn Island, Lloyd had a moment of sheer delight. He'd done it! He'd found out the Headmaster's plan!

But then he remembered that the Headmaster had never been interested in being rich. He didn't want

118

money. He wanted to be in charge of things. How would this factory help him to do that?

Lloyd peered harder as they moved down the corridor. He had to see what was rolling off the machines. The one nearest him had great hoses that came snaking down from the ceiling, squirting something into little plastic pots on a conveyor belt. What was it? Yoghurt?

He couldn't tell, but he managed to see the lids that went on afterwards. Each one had an ape's face printed on it, and a message in spiky letters. EAT APE!

Lloyd blinked. What had that got to do with Hunky Parker?

Further along, a sewing machine was spewing out orange T-shirts, each with the same ugly, snarling ape's face printed above a slogan in heavy black letters.

DON'T MESS WITH APE!

The lunch boxes coming out of the next machine had the same picture too, but the words underneath were different.

WANNA MAKE SOMETHING OF IT?

Lloyd shuddered. Why were all the things so ugly and threatening?

And what were they *for*?

As he was carried on down the corridor, he saw hairy leggings, and pencil sharpeners with bared teeth, and little plastic models with evil faces. Everything was APE!. And the questions rattled round, uselessly, in his head.

What's it all for?

What's the Headmaster up to?

At last they came to the end of the corridor. The man at the front pushed open big double doors and as Lloyd was carried through his head banged on the doorframe, next to the neat little board that said Despatch Department.

The moment they walked in, a Grey Lady marched up to them.

'What are these?'

'Special delivery from Hunky,' said one of the men. 'Carpets, for sending abroad.'

'Carpets?' The Grey Lady's eyebrows rose.

Was there a chance of winning her over? Lloyd twisted his head round and looked into her eyes, as pleadingly as he could. Surely *she* must see they weren't carpets?

The man pulled out the piece of paper that the Headmaster had given him. 'Here are the addresses. It says *Top Security*.'

The Grey Lady snapped to attention and her eyes glazed over. '*The security of the factory is safe in my hands,*' she chanted. Her glance flicked past Lloyd as if he were an object and not a person. 'This one's for Pitcairn Island? It'll take several months by sea. Is that all right?'

The men nodded, and she flicked a hand towards the far side of the warehouse.

120

'That comes under Oceania. Over there.'

Several *months*? Without food or water? Lloyd closed his eyes as the Grey Lady's voice went on, dealing with the others.

'Surinam — that's for South America. Sarawak — Asia. And the one for Burkina Faso goes in the African section.'

They were being sent all over the world. And when they arrived, they would be dead. No one would ever know who they were or what was going on. Lloyd felt hope draining out of him as the men carried him between tall stacks of boxes and dropped him into a long wooden crate on the far side of the warehouse.

They began to pack him round with wood shavings. He closed his eyes, but the wood shavings still tickled his ears and got up his nostrils. From the other side of the warehouse he heard Harvey begin to sneeze, but there was nothing he could do. Mandy's angry grunts were gradually muffled by the wood shavings, and Ian's defiant humming dwindled to nothing.

Then the lids went on.

Even with his eyes closed, Lloyd saw the light disappear as the cover was pushed down on top of him, and from all over the warehouse came the sound of hammering. The lids were being nailed on.

Someone stuck a label on to the side of his crate, with a brisk *slap*, and then the Grey Lady's heels clipped towards him as she came to inspect.

'Excellent!' she said. 'Load the crates on to the lorry.

121

Then you can go to Hunky's office and tell him they will be despatched first thing tomorrow morning.'

Lloyd's crate rocked and tipped as it was lifted on to the men's shoulders. From all over the warehouse, he heard the steady tramp of feet, going through the door and out into the lorry-park.

The crates were stout and strongly-made, and the men didn't treat them gently. Lloyd hit the floor of the lorry with a clang that set his head thudding, and he heard three more clangs, which meant that Harvey and Ian and Mandy weren't being treated any better.

But there was no way of protesting. He had to lie there and listen as the doors of the lorry were fastened and the men walked away.

He let his head flop sideways, feeling the wood shavings scratch his cheek, and he almost despaired. It looked like the end of everything. He was trussed up and addressed to Pitcairn Island, and he couldn't think of anything that could save him.

Chapter 12

HP9

Burkina Faso! Sarawak! Surinam! Pitcairn Island!

Dinah crouched in the control room, listening in total horror as the Headmaster rapped out his orders. Ingrid obviously didn't know where those places were, but she did. And when the Headmaster said *by sea*, she thought she was going to faint.

But he can't! He can't do that to them!

For a second, her eyes blurred and she couldn't concentrate on what was happening at the far end of the studio. Then Ingrid grabbed her plaits, pulling her right to the floor.

'Keep low!' she hissed. 'They're coming!'

Just in time, Dinah ducked under the control desk. The men in brown overalls were marching towards them, with four giant parcels on their shoulders. Long, thin bundles, wrapped in cord from head to foot.

Ingrid gritted her teeth. 'They're not going to get away with this!' she mouthed. 'We'll rescue them!'

Dinah nodded, and huddled closer under the desk with her face jammed against the far wall of the control room.

And that was when she saw it.

HP9.

Her face was level with the bottom of a glass-fronted cupboard, full of neatly-arranged cassettes, and letters on the labels danced in front of her eyes.

HP1: 16/2
HP2: 23/2
HP3:   2/3 . . .

For a second she stared at them vaguely, wondering what they could be. HP1 and HP2 sounded like batteries, but surely they weren't the right shape? She looked further along the shelf.

And saw the cassette labelled HP9: 13/4

HP9 — the thirteenth of April!

That was it! She was certain of it. She was staring at the thing that was going to make people change from Hunky Parker to APE! It was in the cabinet in front of her! If she could find out what it was —

'They're here!' hissed Ingrid in her ear. 'We've got to watch through the door, and see which way they go.'

Dinah nodded, listening to the heavy footsteps as the men in brown overalls marched past with Lloyd and Harvey and Ian and Mandy tied up on their shoulders. But the label on the cassette danced in front of her eyes.

HP9 . . . HP9 . . . 13/4 . . .

When HP9 goes out, the Headmaster had said, *riots will spread all over the country . . . I expect several deaths in that time and considerable destruction of property.*

124

She had to find out what was in that cassette, and when it was going to be used. She *had* to. And she hadn't got long. What else had the Headmaster said?

HP9 will not go out on the thirteenth of April. It will go out — today.

For an instant, craning her head round, Dinah glimpsed Lloyd's eyes, staring grimly out of a cocoon of rope. Then the right hand door of the studio banged shut, and only the Headmaster was left.

He walked down towards the control room, with slow, heavy strides, and the words in Dinah's head followed the rhythm of his steps. H — P — 9 — H — P — 9 —

For one, terrifying moment, she thought he was going to march straight in and discover them lying there. But he was heading for the other door, on the left. His footsteps went past the front of the control room. H — P — 9 —

What *was* it?

The moment the door clicked shut behind the Headmaster, Ingrid was on her feet.

'Come on! The men can't have got far.'

Dinah stood up too, but she was still looking at the cassette. She knew she couldn't just walk away and leave it. She tried the cupboard door, but it was locked. She was just about to try and break the glass, when she remembered the bunch of keys that Ingrid had taken from the Grey Lady's office.

'I'll come in a minute, Ing. Just lend me those keys first, will you?'

Ingrid stared. 'Are you mad? We've got to go *now*!'

'I won't be long.' Dinah took the keys out of her hand and began to try them in the lock. 'I've just got to see what this is.'

'What does it *matter* what it is? I expect it's a rotten Hunky Parker video. Why do you want to look at that?'

A rotten Hunky Parker video . . . Dinah took a deep breath. Suddenly she knew what she was looking at. Unlocking the door, she pulled out the HP9 cassette.

'I can't just go off and leave this,' she said, very quietly. 'It's the ninth Hunky Parker programme. The one that was supposed to go out on the thirteenth of April.'

'So?' Ingrid was too impatient to listen properly.

'So this is what they're going to show tonight. *This is the thing that's going to spark off the riots*.'

'Don't be stupid!' Ingrid was peering through the door, watching which way the men went. 'That'll be at the television studios.'

'No, it won't.' Dinah looked down at the cassette in her hand. 'Don't you remember that article in the paper? About the mysterious woman on the motor bike? She always delivers the Hunky Parker programmes at the last moment. And this is what she's going to be delivering tonight.'

'OK then. Steal it.' Ingrid was still watching the men. 'If it's in your pocket, it can't be on television.'

Dinah was tempted. That would be easy to do. Then they could race straight off, after the others. But . . .

'If we take it,' she said slowly, 'the Headmaster will know there's something wrong. He might even be able to make another tape in time.' She waved a hand at the control desk. 'He's got all the right equipment here.'

Ingrid whirled round. Her eyes were blazing. 'What are you saying? That we *shouldn't* rescue the others? I thought you were a member of SPLAT.'

'Of course I am.' Dinah rubbed her forehead. 'Of *course* I want to rescue them.' She thought of what would happen if they weren't rescued. Of Harvey in a box, on his way to Burkina Faso . . . 'But — '

'But what? Why are we wasting time?' Ingrid had the door open now, and she was half-way through it.

Miserably, Dinah looked across at the control desk. 'Because this is important too. Think of what the Headmaster's planning. Think of what he said about the riots. Maybe I can stop him, if I alter what's on this cassette.'

'If we stay here much longer,' Ingrid said, in a tight, angry voice, 'we shan't have a clue where they've taken the others. We must go now.'

Dinah swallowed. It was the hardest thing she had ever had to say, but she couldn't think what else to do. 'You can follow the others on your own, Ing. You don't need me. I'm staying here.'

For a second, Ingrid stared, with her mouth open. Then she tossed her head. 'Of course I don't need you! We got on all right before you ever came, Dinah Hunter, and we can get on all right without you now!'

She darted through the door, leaving Dinah staring miserably after her, and the faint patter of her feet carried back into the studio as she tiptoed down the corridor. With a sigh, Dinah turned back towards the control room and sat down at the desk.

Taking the cassette out of its box, she slid it into the slot. Then she turned on the computer terminal in front of her. Immediately, a long menu came up on the monitor screen.

1. Dome management
2. Studio utilities
3. Perimeter . . .

She didn't bother to read all the way down. Quickly, she pressed number two, and then she scanned the new menu that appeared.

1. Record tape
2. Wipe tape
3. Mark frames
4. Single frame record
5. Substitute for marked frames
6. Delete marked frames

Until that moment, she hadn't really worked out how she was going to alter the tape, but now she saw how the equipment worked. It let you mark out single frames on the tape and swap them for other frames.

She could almost *see* the Headmaster, bent over the keyboard, making HP9. All he'd had to do was press number four, to record his single frame once. Then he

128

would mark out all the places where he wanted to put it in. And when he pressed number five — POW! The secret, subliminal frames were in the ninth Hunky Parker tape. And it was ready to plunge the country into chaos.

Only he wasn't going to get away with it! Because she was going to mark out his secret frames and delete them.

She knew she was in great danger. Her heart thudded so hard that she could barely think, but she forced herself to ignore it. No use worrying about what could happen if someone came in and found her there. She had to *concentrate*.

Emptying her mind of everything else, she set the tape running and leaned forward to watch. Her right hand was hovering over the keyboard, ready to mark the subliminal frames when she found them.

The programme started just like any other Hunky Parker programme. The huge pig-face filled the screen and Hunky's voice shouted:

'*Who's always right?*'

The answer came back from hundreds of voices, deafeningly loud.

'HUNKY PARKER!'

Then Hunky was waddling into a laundry, waggling his head as he looked up at the heaps of clean washing stacked all round him. He had a bag of soot over his shoulder, and he was eating a toffee apple. And dribbling.

Dinah shuddered, but she kept watching. It didn't

really matter what Hunky did. She was waiting for something else. For the mental shudder that would come, when her mind changed, all on its own.

As Hunky reached the first pile of clean sheets, someone came bounding to meet him. A big, shaggy shape, with long arms and an ugly grin.

'APE!' squealed the pig, patting him with the toffee apple. The ape snarled, and pushed him aside.

And, in that second, Dinah's brain twitched.

Suddenly, Hunky seemed different. He still looked fat and messy and repulsive, but he seemed to have lost all his bounce. He looked boring. Feeble. Bald. *If only he had some hair*, Dinah caught herself thinking. *If only he were tougher*.

That was it! She slammed her finger on to the Stop button, rewound the tape and played it through, frame by frame, searching for the hidden picture. When she found it, there was no mistaking it.

The ape stood in the middle of the picture, a tall figure, dressed in the costume that Ingrid had run off in. But he looked much more terrifying than Ingrid had. The Headmaster's eyes stared through the holes in the snarling mask, glaring straight at Dinah. APE! — OR NOTHING! said the placard in his hand. And under the hairy feet was the familiar Hunky Parker mask, thrown down and empty-eyed.

Hunky Parker is finished, that was what the picture meant. *Now you want this*. And it had worked. Just for a second, as the frame flashed past, Dinah had found herself wanting a character who was strong and fierce and relentless. She had *wanted* APE!

She shuddered. Hunky Parker had seemed like the worst craze possible — but he wasn't. There was an ugly, threatening tilt to the ape's head that promised much more dreadful things.

She remembered the raging crowd that had marched past the bookshop. And the way the children at school had taunted Benedict, for not having any Hunky Parker

things. That was how everything would be, if she didn't somehow fix the HP9 cassette. Only it would be worse, because it would be APE! they wanted.

She jabbed her finger at the keyboard, pressing number three, to mark out the horrible frame. Then she set the tape running again. She had to find all the subliminal frames and mark them out. Then she could press number six, and delete the whole lot.

And the Headmaster's plan would fail!

But she hadn't got very long. It was half-past three already. If the mysterious woman delivered the Hunky Parker tape at half-past five, she'd be leaving quite soon. There wasn't a moment to lose.

Dinah set the tape running and leaned forward again, concentrating on the screen.

Chapter 13

It's the Headmaster!

Trussed up inside the crate, Lloyd was trying, desperately, to fight off panic, and think of something he could *do*. But the cords were rubbing him raw, and his eyes were starting to play tricks on him. Even though he kept them tightly shut, because of the wood shavings, strange lights and colours swirled behind his eyelids.

When he first heard the sounds, he thought his ears were playing tricks too. There was a metallic scraping, like someone undoing the door of the lorry, but it seemed too slow and quiet to be real. And then a long creak, so faint that he could hardly hear it at all. He must be imagining —

And then he heard the footsteps.

They were soft and hesitant, but they were real all right. They came padding round the side of his crate, and someone bumped against a corner. But who? The feet were too slow to be the Grey Lady's. Too light for the men's heavy shoes.

This was a person who didn't want to be heard.

Lloyd tried to wriggle round to knock his head against the side of the crate, but he was much too stiff. All he managed was a jerky shuffle. That was enough though. The footsteps stopped.

133

'Hello?' whispered a voice outside.

At least, Lloyd thought that was what it said. But his ears were muffled and it was difficult to hear. He wriggled harder, thumping his feet against the wood, and the voice muttered again.

Then the lid of the crate began to creak. Slowly, a little bit at a time, someone was levering it off. Friend? Or enemy? Lloyd swallowed and kept very, very still.

With a crunch, the nails came out of the wood. There was a second's pause, and then the lid was lifted. Cautiously, Lloyd opened his eyes and saw a dim light filtering down through the wood shavings. Then, close above his face, a hand slid into the box. He peered upwards, to see who was unpacking him.

And he nearly fainted.

A huge, hairy ape was leaning over the crate, reaching its hand in towards him. Lloyd's eyes widened and he caught his breath so hard that the gag began to choke him.

'Don't be an idiot!' hissed the ape. 'It's me!'

Impatiently, it pulled off its giant ape-hands, which were only gloves. Then it began to untie the gag with small, strong fingers. Lloyd blinked at them as they whisked the gag away.

'Ingrid?'

'Who did you think it was?' the ape snorted impatiently. 'King Kong?'

'I — but we left you at Parker Products. How did you get *here*?'

134

'Same way as you,' said Ingrid, burrowing into the
wood shavings to untie the cords. 'In a lorry.'

'But what about Dinah?'

Ingrid snorted again. 'Don't talk about her! *She*
wouldn't come to save you from being posted. She's still
in that studio, fiddling around with a Hunky Parker
tape.'

Lloyd closed his eyes for a second. He was tired and
hungry, and it all sounded very complicated. But he had
to find out what was going on.

'Get these ropes off me,' he muttered. 'Then you can tell me what's been happening while we untie the others.'

'*Well* — '

It was like unblocking a flood. Once Ingrid started, she hardly stopped to catch her breath. As she and Lloyd let Mandy out and untied Ian, she poured out all sorts of details about workshops and timetables and riots. Lloyd could hardly keep pace with it all.

'You mean — he's going to stop Hunky Parker? And make people want those horrible APE! things?'

Ingrid nodded as they heaved Ian out of his crate. 'Yes. And everyone will go *crazy* because the shops haven't got them.'

'But *why*?' Lloyd stopped, with his hand on the next lid. None of it seemed to make any sense. 'Why would the *Headmaster* want riots? He hates things getting out of control.'

'I don't know — '

Ian coughed. 'Is this a rescue or a discussion group?'

Lloyd scowled, but Mandy put a hand on his arm. 'Ian's right. If we waste too much time talking, we'll never stop the Headmaster. Let's get Harvey out and go and see what Dinah's up to.'

Harvey was very pink in the face when they unwrapped him, but he didn't waste time moaning. 'Let's get out of here and *do* something!' he hissed.

'Forward!' Ian pushed open the door of the lorry. 'And mind the snowdozer.'

'The what?' Lloyd peered past him into the car-park,

bewildered for a moment. Then he saw what Ian meant. Parked right next to them, at the very top of the hill, was the big snowplough that had shunted the snow out of the Dome, when the weather changed to sun. 'Oh, the — '

He meant to say *the snowdozer!* but he was so shaken and tired that it came out wrong.

' — the stownozer.'

'The stone ozer?' Mandy said, behind him. 'What on earth are you talking about?' Then Lloyd jumped down, and she saw the snowplough too. '*Oh*, the — '

But before she could finish, Harvey interrupted, with a nervous giggle. 'The stone ozer! Haven't you ever seen a stone ozer before, Mandy?'

'Ssh!' hissed Lloyd. 'You've got to be *quiet*! We can't afford to get caught again.'

But Harvey couldn't stop, now he'd started. He went on giggling hysterically, and it took them three or four minutes to get him quiet. By that time, Lloyd was looking impatiently at his watch.

It was twenty-past four. And the ninth Hunky Parker programme was due to start at half-past six. They had only just over two hours to stop the Headmaster!

It was almost half-past four by the time they pushed open the studio door. The journey through the factory had been torture. Every time they stopped to hide, Harvey went pink again, and began to mumble, 'Stone ozer!' If he started laughing —

But he managed to hold his giggles back. They reached the studio without being spotted and when they slipped inside the first thing they saw was Dinah, sitting in the control room, her head bent over the desk.

Lloyd called softly. 'Di?'

She glanced up and grinned tensely. 'Nearly ready. I'm just going to check the last few frames of the programme — to make sure there aren't any more hidden pictures. Then all I have to do is press number six here — and they'll be gone. Deleted. That'll fix the Headmaster!'

'Brilliant!' The others wandered up the studio, but Lloyd slid into the control room. 'What are those other monitors, Di? Up by the ceiling?'

Dinah glanced up and shrugged. 'I don't know. Hang on. I'll see if I can switch them on.'

She searched around on the control desk and pressed a couple of keys. Immediately, all the monitors came to life, each showing a different picture. Dinah gave them one quick look.

'Security cameras,' she muttered, and she turned back to what she was doing.

But Lloyd stood and stared at the screens, studying the pictures. Each monitor showed a different part of the building. Two or three had pictures of workshops, where skiers were making clothes or filling yoghurt pots. Lloyd could see the sunbathers and swimmers in the Dome, as well, and the long corridor outside the studio.

There was even a monitor that showed the studio

138

itself. For a moment, Lloyd watched Ian and Harvey and Mandy as they stood round Ingrid, feeling the rough hair of the APE! suit and pulling faces at her mask. All three of them were grinning and teasing her and Lloyd thought he would go and join them.

But then a movement in another of the monitors caught his eye. He glanced at the screen — and saw the figure of Hunky Parker striding down a corridor.

It was the corridor that led to the studio.

For a second, Lloyd was speechless. Then he whirled round. 'It's the Headmaster!' he hissed. 'He's almost here!'

For a split second, the four further down the studio froze completely, paralysed by shock. Ingrid's expression was invisible behind the mask, but Ian, Harvey, and Mandy looked horrified and appalled. Lloyd saw their faces through the glass of the control room and again, on the monitor above his head, and he knew just what they were thinking. *The Headmaster* . . .

In the same second, Dinah jabbed at the keyboard in front of her, trying desperately to finish what she was doing. There was a blinding flash as the lights in the studio turned on, and then off again, and the Hunky Parker cassette whirred in its slot.

'Oh no!' she gasped. 'I hit the wrong key!'

Lloyd's heart sank. 'Are you sure?'

'Certain. I hit number four. Maybe number five too. Single frame record, or substitute, or something. I've messed the whole thing up. I'll have to do it again!'

139

'Don't be daft!' Lloyd grabbed at her wrist. 'There isn't any time. *The Headmaster's coming.*'

He tried to drag her out of the control room, but she pulled herself free.

'Not yet! I can't leave this cassette here.' She switched off, ejected the cassette and slid it back into its case. Then she jammed it into the cabinet, locked the door and pulled out the keys.

But she hadn't got a proper grip on the keys. When Lloyd tugged at her arm again, the whole bunch fell out of her hand and slid under the control desk.

'Come *on!*' Lloyd didn't give her a chance to get them back. He pulled her out of the control room and pushed her down behind one of the scenery screens as the right hand door of the studio opened.

In marched the Headmaster. He glanced towards the left hand door. From behind it came the sound of sharp, metal heels clicking down the corridor.

Lloyd held his breath.

The left hand door opened and in marched a Grey Lady.

'You are twenty seconds late,' the Headmaster's voice said coldly.

'I'm sorry, Hunky.'

'Are you ready to leave?'

'Yes, sir.' The Grey Lady was dressed in heavier overalls than usual, and she was carrying a motorcycle helmet. 'The bike is outside, ready to start.'

'Then I shall overlook your lateness, as long as it is not

140

repeated.' The Headmaster nodded and walked into the control room. Peering from behind the screen, Lloyd saw him take some keys out of his pocket and unlock the door. He pulled out the cassette that Dinah had just replaced.

HP9.

It was going off to the television studio now. They'd missed their chance to alter it. In two hours, everyone in the country would be watching that tape.

And when it finished, the riots would begin.

'Go straight to the studio,' said the icy voice from behind the pig mask, 'and deliver the cassette to Mr Jessop. Personally.'

'Yes, Hunky.'

'Then wait to collect it afterwards. Bring it back here immediately.'

Nodding, the Grey Lady pushed the cassette into her pocket and pulled on the helmet. Then she marched out of the left hand door and they heard her feet clicking down the corridor.

The Headmaster turned the other way, towards the right hand door. But, as he went, he glanced round quickly, and something caught his eye. Something in the control room. He stepped back in and bent down to pick it up.

For a second, Lloyd couldn't work out what it was. But Dinah guessed. He saw her go white.

When the Headmaster straightened, he was holding the bunch of keys that she had dropped.

Chapter 14

Escape

Even then, things might have been all right. If it hadn't been for Harvey.

Dinah saw him go pale when the Headmaster walked into the studio, and she kept glancing round, to make sure he was all right. He was blinking nervously, but he stayed very still and quiet until the Headmaster picked up the keys.

Then he panicked.

With a squeal, he darted out from behind the scenery screen, heading for the right hand door. Mandy tried to hold him back, but it was no use. He wrenched himself free and ran on.

With two quick strides, the Headmaster was out of the control room. In another moment he would have grabbed Harvey. But Ingrid gave a fierce yell.

'Oh no, you *don't*!'

She shot out of her hiding place like a hairy brown hurricane, her arms waving above her head. The Headmaster was so startled that, for a second, he hesitated. That gave Harvey enough time to shoot through the door and out of the studio. But it left Ingrid in danger.

'You idiot!' muttered Mandy. 'We'll have to — oh, come *on*, Ian!'

The two of them charged out as well, heading in different directions. Suddenly the room seemed full of flying SPLAT members, each one trying to draw the Headmaster away from the others.

Dinah would have run too, but Lloyd caught her arm. 'Don't be silly!' he whispered. 'He doesn't know you and Ingrid are here. He'll think it's me wearing the APE! suit. If we hide, we can stay free and help the others.'

It was hard to go on crouching behind the screen while the others were running wildly, but Dinah could see he was right. She sat very still, watching Mandy follow Harvey out of the right hand door, while Ian and Ingrid went the other way.

The Headmaster didn't make any attempt to chase them. As they vanished, he marched into the control room, shutting the door behind him. Peering round the screen, Dinah could see him, through the glass. He was bending over the control desk, flicking buttons.

After a few seconds, he picked up a microphone and suddenly they heard his voice. It came booming through the doors, from loudspeakers in the corridors.

'We have intruders in The Sty. Two in the West Section and two in the East Section. I have autolocked all outside doors, so that no one can leave the building.'

He glanced up at the monitors above the desk, and a cold, tight smile spread across his face. Dinah shuddered.

'Capture will present no problems,' she heard him say. 'One intruder is dressed as an ape and the other three are

143

wearing standard Hunky Parker ski suits. They are all extremely agitated. We shall apply Procedure Forty-Two.'

Dinah and Lloyd looked at each other. They could hear the message resounding along the corridor, and they guessed there must be loudspeakers all over the building. How could Harvey and the others possibly escape?

The Headmaster obviously thought they couldn't. He stood up to leave, bending forward to speak his final message into the microphone.

'I expect Total Intruder Clearance within five minutes. When you have captured the intruders, they are to be brought to my office. I shall wait for them there.'

With a final chilly smile at the monitors, he put down the microphone and strode out of the studio. Dinah looked desperately at Lloyd.

'What are we going to do?'

'Let's have a look at those monitors. We might be able to see what's going on.'

They tore across to the control room and stared up at the screens. Ian, Mandy, and Ingrid were easy to see.

Ian was running between rows of skiers, all frantically making tracksuits. Not one of the skiers glanced his way, but dozens of printed APE! faces snarled up at him, and three Grey Ladies were racing down the rows, moving to head him off.

Mandy was in the yoghurt-packing workshop, surrounded by ugly cartons with rims like jagged teeth.

Four men in brown overalls were chasing her, but she was very nimble, and she kept darting out of sight behind the machines. But she couldn't hide for long. There were screens in the workshops too, high up on the walls, and every time the men lost track of her they could glance up and see where she was.

Ingrid was in a workshop full of flexes. They hung down from the ceiling in rows, connecting the electricity supply to the benches, where sweating skiers were making hairy leotards. As Lloyd and Dinah watched, Ingrid grabbed a flex, pushed off with her feet and swung across to the next one. And then the next. And the next. There was no sound from the monitors, but her mouth was wide open, behind the ape mask, and Dinah knew she was yelling.

And where was Harvey?

One of the other monitors showed a Grey Lady and two men in brown overalls. They were obviously hunting for someone, because the Grey Lady kept looking up at the screen on the wall and then ordering the men to peer under machines. But who were they hunting? All Dinah could see was dozens of skiers. Rows of plastic ketchup bottles, that said *Get APE! Squirt!* But no Harvey.

Then she spotted him. Just for a second, his round face peered out from one of the machines. He was in the space underneath, which was too small for the men to get into, and he was wriggling round the workshop, at top speed.

Lloyd pulled a face. 'They're all in different places. And they'll never escape unless we get the outside doors

145

unlocked. Can you work out how to switch off the autolock, Di?'

'I can try.' Dinah looked down at the keyboard. 'It must be possible to work it out. Maybe I should — '

'Do whatever you like. Just *hurry*!'

Sitting down in front of the controls, Dinah began to tap the keys. There must be a Master Program somewhere. A set of instructions that controlled the whole building. If only she could find it . . .

Lloyd was breathing down her neck, rattling his knuckles impatiently against the back of her chair. The moment she called up a menu, he began to read it aloud.

'1 — Dome management. 2 — Studio utilities. 3 — Perimeter — We want Dome management don't we?' Before Dinah could say anything, he had leaned over her shoulder and pressed number one. Immediately, a page of figures appeared on the screen.

Dinah frowned. 'That's not it. Those are all times and temperatures.'

Lloyd peered at them and snorted impatiently. 'Must be for swapping the snow and the sun, inside the Dome. How do I get back to the menu? Space bar?'

He held it down, without waiting for a reply.

Dinah pushed him out of the way. 'Why don't you leave things alone? That's not how you get the menu. All you've done is wipe out the bit at the beginning, that said *eight hours*. Now I'll have to type it back in.'

'We haven't got time for that!' Lloyd jabbed at the keyboard again, and this time the figures vanished and the menu reappeared. 'Try Perimeter Control.'

Dinah bit her lip. There was no point in arguing with him. It was better to find the autolock herself, before he did something *really* stupid. She elbowed him out of the way and got going on Perimeter Control.

A couple of seconds later, she had found the autolock, and was typing Off.

'There you are.' She leaned back. 'Done it! The doors are unlocked.'

'At last.' Lloyd picked up the microphone. 'Do you think the others will hear if I talk through this?'

Dinah nodded. 'I expect so. If you switch on. What are you going to do?'

Lloyd took a deep breath. 'I'm going to tell the others where to meet us. But it's got to be a secret message.' He flicked the microphone switch and raised his voice. 'Calling SPLAT! Calling SPLAT!'

Dinah heard the words echoing from the loudspeakers outside. That meant the message was going all over the building. So the others would hear it all right — but she and Lloyd were in danger now. As soon as the Headmaster heard Lloyd's voice, he would know they were in the studio. They had to hurry.

'Forget everything the Headmaster said,' Lloyd boomed. 'Put the video cameras out of action, if you can. Then head straight for — for *the stone ozer*. We'll meet you there.'

'The stone *what*?' Dinah stared.

Lloyd didn't waste time explaining. Dropping the

microphone, he glanced up at the monitors over their heads. The pictures were beginning to disappear.

Ian had grabbed a handful of tracksuits and flung them at the video camera which pointed his way. They snagged on the corners, and the screen was covered by a blurred, snarling face.

Ingrid was standing on a workbench. She seized the nearest flex and pushed off, swinging fast. For a second, Dinah glimpsed her eyes, fierce and determined, through the holes in the mask. Then she swung towards the camera, feet first. There was a crash, and the monitor went blank.

Mandy ducked round one of the yoghurt-packing machines, to the side where the controls were. She stopped for a second and flicked two levers, and the machine went mad. Instead of feeding yoghurt cartons neatly into shrink wrap, it began to hurl them high into the air, towards the camera. SLURP! A second later, all Dinah and Lloyd could see was thick white trickles, running from top to bottom of the screen.

Then Harvey shot out from underneath a conveyor belt, fifty metres away from the people who were chasing him. Grabbing two plastic ketchup bottles, he wrenched the tops off, pointed at the camera and squirted. Two jets of scarlet shot out, and the picture vanished in a bright red haze.

Lloyd grinned at Dinah and grabbed her hand. 'Come on! We've got to get there too.'

'Get *where*?'

'To the stone ozer, of course. Come on! The Head-master went that way, so we'll go this way.'

He hauled her through the left hand door, into a long, grey corridor. Down at the far end was a line of warehouse trolleys, stacked with cardboard boxes. Lloyd gave a whoop of delight.

'Brilliant! That's just what we need.'

'Trolleys? Whatever for?'

'For transport, of course. And ammunition. Come on.'

Dinah didn't understand, but Lloyd didn't wait to explain. Racing down the corridor, he grabbed hold of the nearest trolley and swung it to the left.

'Let's go!'

The cardboard boxes on the trolley were stacked higher than his head and he had to peer round them to see where he was going, but that didn't slow him down. He began to run along the next corridor, pushing the trolley in front of him. It gathered speed quickly on the smooth floor.

When it was going really fast, he jumped on to the back, leaning from side to side to steer and putting a foot to the ground from time to time to push it along faster.

'Fantastic!' Dinah grabbed a trolley for herself and set off after him.

They hadn't gone far before two men in brown overalls burst out of a room a little way ahead of them. They stood side by side in the middle of the corridor, blocking the way.

But they didn't catch Lloyd. His trolley cannoned

straight into them, hitting them so hard that they went flying. He scooted on without stopping and Dinah rattled up behind.

She put her hand into the nearest cardboard box, to see what her trolley was carrying, and pulled out a cardboard carton with lurid red writing on it.

Grrr — APE! Juice!
It's wild!

Grinning, she flung the carton straight at the men as they began to scramble to their feet. It missed them, but it hit the wall and burst, spraying purple grape juice everywhere.

'And again!' yelled Lloyd, from in front, throwing two more cartons.

The men ducked down, shielding their faces, and Dinah swished past untouched.

Lloyd was nearly at the end of the corridor. 'Which way?' he called. 'Right or left?'

Dinah frowned, working out where they were. 'Right!' she yelled back. 'There ought to be a door that way.'

Without stopping his trolley, Lloyd leaned right, sticking out his left foot to push himself round as he got close to the wall. Dinah was just getting ready to do the same, when she heard him shout.

'Grey Ladies! And — oh, *help*!'

Dinah whisked round the corner, and her eyes widened in horror. She had been right about the door.

150

There was one straight ahead. But in between them and the door stood four Grey Ladies.

And a barricade.

The Grey Ladies had pulled desks and filing cabinets out of the offices on either side, and blocked off the whole corridor. The barricade was a couple of metres high, and it stretched back for twice that length. There was no chance of knocking it down.

Lloyd stopped pushing his trolley, but Dinah didn't. She was frantically doing sums in her head. If they went fast enough . . . with the weight of the trolleys . . . and the force of the impact . . . they might just . . .

She leaned sideways as she drew level with Lloyd. 'We'll have to go over!' she muttered. 'Get your trolley moving *really* fast and then climb up on top of the boxes.'

They began to scoot along the ground towards the Grey Ladies, building up speed. When the trolleys were thundering and swaying down the corridor, Dinah nodded, and she and Lloyd scrambled up on top of the boxes, crouching low so that they stayed hidden.

The Grey Ladies didn't see them. Grinning confidently, they stepped apart to let the trolleys hit the barricade. Dinah gritted her teeth. Not yet. Not yet. They'd spoil it all if they moved too soon.

The barricade loomed closer and closer.

Not yet. Not yet . . .

She left it until they were almost there, and then she hissed at Lloyd. 'Now!'

Rising to their feet, they ran forward, on top of the

151

boxes, just as the trolleys crashed into the heap of furniture. The force of the crash flung them forwards, right over the barricade. They slid down the far side and headed for the door.

'You won't get away,' yelled the Grey Ladies. 'The door is autolocked!'

'That's what you think!' muttered Lloyd. 'Come on, Di!'

They flung themselves at the door, pushing the handle down — and it opened. Now it was the Grey Ladies who were trapped behind the barricade. Dinah heard their high heels scraping on wood as they tried to scramble over.

'Quick!' she gasped. 'Before they make it!'

She dashed through the door and found herself in the

car-park where the lorries were. She looked round wildly.

'Where are we going?'

'Stone . . . ozer . . .' panted Lloyd. 'Over . . . there.'

For a second, Dinah thought he had gone mad. Then she saw the huge snowplough parked at the top of the slope.

'Oh, the *snowdozer*!'

'All I could think of. I was hoping the others . . . would be there already. But we'll have . . . to wait.'

Lloyd took a step towards the snowplough. And then stopped dead. Because it had begun to move. Slowly but surely, the huge machine was rolling down the hill towards them.

'B-but that's impossible,' stuttered Dinah. 'There's no one in it!'

Chapter 15

The Last Chance

'Of course there's someone in it!' hissed a scornful voice. Ingrid's head popped up behind the windscreen. 'Where did you *think* we were?'

'But — ' Lloyd stared. 'You all escaped?'

Ian peered over Ingrid's shoulder, grinning. 'They thought the stone ozer was something to do with getting stones out of cherries. So they went haring off to the fruit-canning workshop. And we sneaked out here.'

'But — ' Lloyd was still startled. 'Are you *driving* that thing?'

'Get *in*!' Ingrid said impatiently. 'Don't let them catch us.'

The snowplough rolled closer, and Lloyd saw Mandy, hunched low behind the steering wheel. She grinned at him.

'We can't turn on the engine, because we haven't got the keys. But we've taken off the handbrake — and it's downhill all the way to the gates. Once we really get rolling, no one will be able to stop this thing.'

'All we've got to do is find a phone!' said Ingrid. 'If we phone the television studios before half-past six — '

' — *we can stop Hunky Parker Nine!*' Harvey bounced up and down on the back seat. 'It's not too late! We can still beat the Headmaster!'

'But we haven't found the phone *yet*,' drawled Ian. 'So you'd better get in fast. Put your foot on the brake, Ing.'

Ingrid pressed the pedal and Dinah and Lloyd scrambled in as the snowplough slowed down. It wasn't built to carry six people, but Dinah squashed in on top of Harvey and Ian, and Lloyd pushed his way into the driving seat, edging Mandy closer to Ingrid.

'Let's go!' he hissed, grabbing the steering wheel.

Ingrid took her foot off the brake and the snowplough began to move again, gathering speed very quickly because it was so heavy.

They rolled silently down the car-park, towards the buildings. Immediately ahead of them was the Welcome Suite, and behind it the glass walls of the Dome, glittering in the evening sunlight.

On either side of the Dome, the ground dropped away. To the right, the slope was covered with the grey, sprawling mass of the factory block. To the left were rows of bright little holiday chalets, scattered all the way down the hill. There was a road in each direction.

But which was the way out?

Lloyd glanced at the clock on the dashboard. Five fifteen. Only an hour and a quarter until the start of Hunky Parker Nine. They should be able to reach a phone in time to stop it. But only if he didn't make a mistake. Which way . . .?

He was so busy staring at the roads that he didn't even glance at the Dome. It was Ingrid who gasped, as they came out from behind the Welcome Suite.

'Look! Look what's happening!'

At the same moment, Mandy grabbed Lloyd's arm. 'Stop! We've got to *do* something!'

'What — ?' All the others were pointing now. Lloyd lifted his eyes and looked at the Dome.

It had gone crazy.

From outside, it looked like a child's snowstorm that had been shaken roughly. The air was full of flying flakes of snow, so thick that Lloyd could hardly make out the figures inside. But he saw enough to know that something was wrong. There were plenty of people in ski suits, but weren't some people wearing . . . *swimming costumes*?

In the middle of the snowflakes, potted plants and sunloungers were rising out of the floor. And a jet of water shot down the water slide, freezing into icicles as it fell.

SNOW TOMORROW, SUN TODAY, said the big notice on the end wall. But the wall hadn't stopped. The whistle sounded, and it went on rotating SUN TOMORROW, SNOW TODAY . . .

More skiers crowded into the Dome, blocking the entrances at the back, so the sunbathers couldn't get out. Lloyd could see hundreds of people squashed together, struggling to move.

Harvey blinked. 'What's happening?'

'Everything's speeded up!' Mandy sounded horrified. 'It's changing, like it did before, but there's no break in between. So all the people have got squashed in together.'

156

'But why?' murmured Ian. 'Who did it?'

Dinah gulped. 'I think — oh, Lloyd, *we* did! Remember when you pressed the space bar on the computer? You wiped out the eight hour delay.'

The whistle sounded once more, and they saw the wall rotate again, spinning round to the other side.

Skiers and sunbathers were crammed in together, without any room to escape. And still the bell was ringing and the wall was turning, faster and faster. No one could get out that way now. It was spinning continuously, so quickly that the words blurred into nonsense.

. . . SUNTODAYSNOWTODAYSUNTODAY . . .

Snowflakes whirled away from the blowers at double speed, filling half the dome with a blizzard. But, where they hit the heaters, they changed into boiling steam that billowed back at the holidaymakers. In between, a thick blanket of fog began to form, broken by the jets of icy water from the water slide.

People were elbowing their way towards the entrance, but there was no way out there either. The doors opened inwards and the pressure of the crowd had jammed them shut. Children were shivering and crying, frozen sunbathers were trying to share ski jackets, and drenched skiers were stifling in the steam.

'We've got to stop,' Mandy said desperately. 'We've got to help them!' She slid forward in the seat and jammed her foot down on to the foot brake.

157

'We can't!' Lloyd tried to kick her foot away. 'Look at the clock. We haven't got time!'

They all glanced up at the giant pig-clock on the front of the Dome. The right nostril flickered, as another minute clicked past, and the black numbers in the snout loomed threateningly.

17:20

Lloyd *knew* they had to go on. 'If we stop the plough now, we'll probably get caught. And even if we don't, we'll run out of time. We'll be too late to ring the television studios.'

'I can't help that.' Mandy jammed her foot down harder and tugged at the handbrake. 'You go on if you like, but I'm going to help these poor people. They could *die*!'

Standing up on the seat, she stepped over Ingrid and jumped out of the snowplough. Before anyone could stop her, she was running across the grass, towards the Dome.

'She's right,' Dinah said grimly. '*We* did that to those people, Lloyd. We've got to rescue them. Come on. If we hurry, we might have time to find a phone as well.'

'But — ' For a second, Lloyd stayed where he was, watching the others scramble out. Should he go on by himself? It would only take one person to phone the television studios.

Then he saw Mandy fling herself uselessly against the solid glass doors of the Dome, and he knew he couldn't leave. The others hadn't got a *clue*. He was the only person with enough sense to organize a rescue.

158

Jumping out of the plough, he ran towards the Dome. 'It's no use doing it on your own,' he called. 'We've got to hit the doors *together*. And the people inside have to stop pushing.'

Mandy looked round, not quite sure what he meant, but Dinah got the idea at once. She put her face against the doors and yelled. 'Step back! Just enough to let us push. *Please!*'

Some of the holidaymakers understood. The ones in front called back over their shoulders to the people behind and slightly — very slightly — the crowd shifted.

It was enough. It *had* to be enough. 'NOW!' yelled Lloyd.

All six of them charged straight at the doors, throwing their weight against the glass. And the doors gave way.

It was like uncorking a bottle. Immediately, people started to pour out of the Dome, raging and gasping and sobbing with relief. They might have been hypnotized before, but they were wide awake now. Wide awake and furious.

'It shouldn't be allowed!'

'Where's the manager?'

'We don't want the manager. We want the police!'

'We want — '

Lloyd looked at the angry faces. Then he looked up at the clock. It was still before half-past five. If he could persuade *all* these people to go looking for telephones, someone was bound to find one in time. He took a deep breath, ready to shout above the noise.

But before he could say a word — everything inside the Dome stopped.

The blowers were still, the heaters shut off and the end wall ground to a halt, half-way round. The shouts died away as people turned round to look, puzzled and speechless. Nothing moved, except the last few flakes of snow, fluttering to the floor, and there was no sound except the steady drip, drip, drip of melting ice.

Then, from way overhead, the whistle sounded once more and a great voice came booming down from the loudspeakers.

'Nobody is to move! You are all feeling sleepy. Very, very sleepy . . .'

'No!' whispered Harvey. 'No! Don't listen to him!'

But it was too late. The holidaymakers had been hypnotized in the Welcome Suite, when they first came to The Sty. Now they had no choice and they obeyed automatically. Lloyd saw their eyes close and their faces grow blank as they turned towards the loudspeakers. Waiting to be told what to do.

'Quick!' he shouted. 'We've got to get away. NOW!'

He led the dash to the snowplough, with the others close behind him. But they could hear the Headmaster's voice booming above their heads.

'There is a snowplough beside the Dome. You will all go and surround it. It must not be permitted to move, and the people in it must not be allowed to escape. Is that clear?'

The reply came from all over the crowd. Hundreds of

160

people, speaking in the same dead, mechanical voices, exactly together.

'Yes, Hunky.'

'Quick! Quick!' screamed Ingrid, throwing herself into the front seat. 'I'll take the handbrake off!'

She wrenched at it, while the others were still leaping in, and Lloyd spun the wheel to the right, as the snowplough began to roll. Perhaps they could still make it. Perhaps . . .

But it was no use. The crowd surged forward from the Dome, spreading all round them. Dozens of people — men, women, and children — stepped straight in front of the snowplough.

'Brake!' shrieked Mandy. 'We're going to run them over!'

'They'll have to get out of the way!' Lloyd said desperately.

But he knew they couldn't. They were hypnotized and they would do exactly what the Headmaster had told them to. And, even if the first people got run over, there were more behind them. And more behind that.

There wasn't a hope of getting through.

Grimly, he jammed his foot down and pulled on the handbrake. As the snowplough stopped, he made one, desperate effort to escape, but the moment he stood up he was pushed down by dozens of hands. The holidaymakers were obeying the Headmaster's orders. Exactly. They weren't going to let any of the children out.

161

Sinking back into his seat, Lloyd looked round at the hundreds of blank, dull faces. There was nothing to be done. They could only wait, for whatever the Head-master had planned. He turned and stared at the ugly, triumphant pig-face on the front of the Dome, and watched the minutes ticking away. On and on and on.

17:32
17:33 . . .

*   *   *

They were still sitting there, almost an hour later, when the numbers clicked to the time they'd all been dreading.

18:30

Immediately, a great voice came booming out from the Dome. 'YES, FOLKS, THAT'S IT! IT'S HUNKY PARKER TIME!'

Trumpets blared, and the crowd behind the snowplough began to separate, leaving a narrow path through from the Dome. Down the path, walking very slowly, came a tall figure in a pig-mask.

He paced steadily towards them, his sea-green eyes flaming through the holes in the mask like frozen lightning. Lloyd stared back defiantly, waiting to hear what he would say.

But the Headmaster didn't say anything. Not for fifteen minutes. He walked up to the snowplough and stood watching the clock on the Dome as the numbers changed. Until they reached six forty-five, he was completely silent.

Then he did speak, rapping out the words so fiercely that even Ingrid didn't dare to argue.

'Take off that APE! suit!'

She pulled off the mask and the big, hairy suit and handed them over, and the Headmaster turned to face the crowd.

'*What do you see?*'

The reply came back mechanically, from hundreds of throats.

'*We see what Hunky tells us.*'

The Headmaster nodded and raised a hand. 'Close your eyes. When you open them, Hunky will be gone. And you will see your new master.'

Obediently, all the holidaymakers closed their eyes. Only the six children in the snowplough went on watching as the Headmaster's hands reached slowly up towards the Hunky Parker mask.

He lifted it off, and they saw the face they had hoped never to see again. The colourless hair, the paper-white skin, and the huge, terrible eyes. The Headmaster gazed

164

across at them, and his mouth curled into a triumphant smile.

'I have succeeded,' he said softly. 'Hunky Parker is finished — and tomorrow the whole country will be in chaos! People will be smashing and looting and rioting in the streets.'

'But *why?*' Lloyd gripped the steering wheel and glared up at him. 'I thought you hated things like that.'

The Headmaster's thin lips twisted cruelly. 'Not if they are useful. And these riots will be. Because only one person will be able to stop them. The man who has what they want!'

Lloyd gasped, 'The APE! goods! *That's* what they're for!'

'Correct.' The Headmaster smiled even more unpleasantly. 'When enough damage has been done, I shall stop the riots — *and I shall take over the country!*'

'But you can't — ' faltered Mandy.

'I can, and I shall!' thundered the Headmaster. 'I shall take over everything. And there will be no more riots. No more crazes. No more *choosing*.' He lifted his head, and his voice rang out over The Sty. '*I* shall decide what people need, and I shall *make* them want it. They will produce it themselves, in my factories, with no nonsense about wages. And they will think — ' his lip curled scornfully ' — that they are on holiday.'

Dinah twisted her fingers together. 'It'll be a country of slave-robots, all making things for each other. What's the point of that?'

165

'Efficiency,' the Headmaster said icily.

He pulled on the hairy suit and dropped the great, ugly mask on to his head. Lloyd shuddered. The costume had looked bad enough on Ingrid, but at least it had been baggy, and faintly comic. Now it was terrifying.

The Headmaster turned to face the holidaymakers. 'Open your eyes!' he said.

Hundreds of eyes opened, staring blankly and obediently at the enormous ape. And he glared back at them.

'I am APE! *What do you see?*'

Lloyd clenched his fists. Surely it couldn't be that easy? *Surely* the crowd couldn't just change . . . ? But the answer came back without a second's hesitation.

'*We see what APE! tells us.*'

Chapter 16

We Want APE!

Ingrid leapt to her feet. 'Don't be silly! It's all a trick!'

The holidaymakers stared back, with smooth, untroubled faces, and the Headmaster shook his huge, masked head.

'You are wasting your breath. They do not even hear you.'

'Well, other people will!' Harvey said fiercely. 'We'll tell everyone what you're up to!'

The Headmaster turned and looked at him. 'I don't think so,' he murmured. 'I have . . . other plans for you.'

'Other plans?' Harvey went pale.

'I am going to send you to the Chill Room.'

None of them knew what he meant, but the way he said it made them shudder. Dinah lifted her chin and stared past him, avoiding his eyes.

'What's the Chill Room?'

'Where the snow is stored when it is not needed in the Dome.' The Headmaster gave a small, unpleasant chuckle. 'I think you will find it . . . fatally cold.'

He turned away, towards the holidaymakers, and raised his voice to reach the very edge of the huge crowd.

'*What do you see?*'

'*We see what APE! tells us.*'

'What you see is the Dome.' The Headmaster stepped away from the snowplough and his massive, hairy arm pointed towards the glass walls. 'At the front is a door . . .'

The holidaymakers turned, their glazed eyes following his finger, and he began to give instructions. Lloyd and the others listened, their eyes widening in horror as the Headmaster explained how they were to be shut up in the giant freezer.

But Dinah hardly heard. The Headmaster's first words were still ringing in her head. *What you see is the Dome . . .*

He had made a mistake! The holidaymakers saw only what he told them — and he hadn't said a word about snowploughs or children. For a few seconds, at least, the six of them would be invisible to everyone in the crowd!

Dinah nudged Ian and Harvey. '*Come on!*' she mouthed. '*We can go.*'

The Headmaster was still giving instructions, with his back turned. Like shadows, they slid out of the snowplough, pushing their way between people in swimming costumes and people in ski suits. No one took any notice at all. *We see what APE! tells us . . .*

Creeping on tiptoe, Dinah moved clear of the crowd and began to lead the way down the drive. But she was keeping an eye on the Headmaster. As soon as he began to turn back, she yelled.

'Run!'

Grabbing Harvey's hand, she threw herself forward.

They all sprinted down the drive, their eyes fixed on the gate that led out to the road. It was only two hundred metres away. But the Headmaster didn't mean to let them reach it.

'Bring those children back!' he shouted.

All together, the holidaymakers turned and began to run. Dinah glanced back, and shuddered at what she saw. There was a wall of people sprinting down the drive. Running with expressionless faces, like robots who would never tire.

Harvey moaned, gasping for breath, but she tugged him on. 'Don't stop! We can make it if we run!'

For a moment he believed her, and she felt him surge forward. But then his face changed, and he pointed down the drive, towards the gate.

'It's no good, Di. We can't get out. There's people coming the other way, too!'

Ingrid had seen them as well. 'Look!' she shrieked. 'What are we going to do?'

Dozens of cars were driving through the gateway, two or three at a time, and behind them were more. The line stretched as far as Dinah could see.

And the people inside the cars were chanting. Shouting the same words over and over again, at the tops of their voices. For a second, Dinah couldn't make out what they were saying, but when she did, her heart sank.

'WE WANT APE! WE WANT APE! WE WANT APE!'

169

If they were shouting that, they must have seen HP9. The Headmaster's plan was working.

'Don't give up!' bellowed Lloyd. 'Let's go and talk to them!' He went racing towards the cars.

'No!' shouted Dinah. 'They might be dangerous —'

But he didn't listen. He ran on and, after a moment's hesitation, Dinah and the others raced after him. Even if it was dangerous, they were still SPLAT. They stuck together.

As they drew level with the first car, it slowed down, to avoid hitting them. Without waiting for an invitation, Lloyd wrenched the rear door open and dived in. Dinah pulled Harvey after him, and the other three tumbled in too, squashed into the back seat.

There was a shrill shriek from the little girl in front. 'Uncle Gareth!'

The driver glanced over his shoulder, frowning. 'What's going on?'

Ingrid leaned forward, and gripped the front seat. 'There's an . . . an ape up there, and he's trying to get us.'

The little girl shrieked again. 'WE WANT APE!'

'We certainly do,' her uncle said grimly.

They were driving through the holidaymakers now, but that was no problem. *Bring those children back*, the Headmaster had said — and here they were, coming back on their own. So the crowd just parted to let them through.

Uncle Gareth was looking from side to side, peering

through the bushes. 'Where *is* APE!' he muttered. 'That's who we've come for.'

Dinah swallowed. 'Why do you want him?'

'Because — ' Uncle Gareth looked confused. ' — because I saw him on the Hunky Parker programme just now. And he's wicked. He has to be stopped.'

Dinah stared. 'The programme made you think *that*?'

'Oh, what does it matter about the rotten old programme?' Ingrid leaped up, pointing through the windscreen. 'There he is!'

Straight ahead of them, in the middle of the road, was the snowplough. And standing on the bonnet, facing them down the drive, was the tall figure of the Headmaster in his mask and costume.

APE!

Uncle Gareth's foot faltered on the pedal, and Dinah heard the chant behind them die away, as the sea-green eyes stared out over the cars. The Headmaster's voice boomed down the drive.

'I am APE! and this is The Jungle! You must be feeling sleepy after your journey . . .'

No! thought Dinah. *He mustn't hypnotize them!* She wound down the window and yelled, as loudly as she could.

'THAT'S APE! GET HIM!'

The Headmaster was startled. For an instant, he stopped speaking, and in that instant, Uncle Gareth opened his mouth and yelled, ferociously.

'GET APE! GET APE!'

Immediately, the shout was repeated, from every car in the drive. The Headmaster's voice was drowned by the noise.

For a split second, he glared down at Dinah. Then he turned and leapt into the driving seat of the snowplough. With a roar, the engine started, and he swung the steering wheel, turning off the road, towards the Dome.

'Oh no, you don't, my boyo!' Grimly, Uncle Gareth spun his own wheel. 'We've got things to sort out with you!'

But he hadn't noticed the motor bike coming up behind him, weaving its way between the cars. As he swung left, he caught it, broadside on, and it clattered over on to its side. The Grey Lady riding it was flung sprawling on to the grass and a small black box flew out of her pocket.

Uncle Gareth jammed on his brakes and leapt out of the car, bending over her as she lifted her dazed head. 'Are you all right?'

Dinah leapt out too, but not to look after the Grey Lady. Her eyes were on the little black box. It was the cassette. HP9. She was sure of it.

'Don't waste time!' bellowed Lloyd. 'The Headmaster's driving into the Dome! What's he up to?'

He jumped out of the car and began to race after the snowplough. Jamming the cassette into her pocket, Dinah ran too, with the rest of SPLAT close behind.

When people saw what they were doing, they leapt out of the cars and followed, still keeping up the same steady

172

chant. 'GET APE! GET APE!' Dinah and the others were well ahead, but even so, by the time they reached the Dome the snowplough was already over at the far side, disappearing through the gap at the side of the swivelling wall.

'Follow him!' Lloyd yelled. 'He mustn't get away!'

The six of them charged across the Dome, slithering in half-melted snow, and slipping on the trampled leaves of tropical plants. When they reached the gap, they ran straight through, in the tracks of the snowplough.

Before anyone else could catch up, the huge wall began to turn, closing the space they had come through.

'We'll be trapped!' squealed Harvey. 'Get out!'

'We can't,' Lloyd said grimly. '*We've got to know what the Headmaster's doing.* Come on.' He dragged Harvey through, just as the gap finally closed.

They were alone in a small grey lobby, with no way of turning back.

Ahead, down a short corridor, they could see the first of the workshops, but the tracks of the snowplough did not go that way. They turned left, through a door labelled Chill Room.

Lloyd didn't hesitate. 'Come on!'

Tugging the heavy door open, he led the way — into a giant snowdrift. The huge, high room was packed with snow, from floor to ceiling. Through the middle was a narrow corridor, made by the snowplough, with great white walls, six metres high.

'It's *cold*!' wailed Harvey. 'My nose is going blue!'

'Try running,' drawled Ian. 'That'll warm you up.'

But he was wrong. They raced between the white walls at top speed, but by the time they reached the far side they were all shivering uncontrollably.

'W-what's in there?' said Ingrid. They were staring at another huge closed door. Tropical Room, it said.

'Only one w-way to find out,' shivered Lloyd.

He pushed the door open — and instantly the shivers disappeared. They were sweltering.

It was like being in a greenhouse. The room was stacked with hundreds of lush green plants — the ones that decorated the Dome when it was sunny. The hot air was misty and damp, and huge green leaves spread everywhere.

Except in the very centre of the room. There the snowplough had crashed a way through, leaving a slimy trail of shattered pots and mashed, ruined leaves.

'That's where he went!' Without waiting to discuss it with the rest of them, Lloyd raced along the snowplough's track, towards yet another door, on the far side of the room.

Dinah felt horribly uneasy. She wanted to stop for a second. To think about what they were getting into. But Ingrid and Ian were already well ahead of her, and even Harvey was so excited that he had forgotten to be afraid. Gritting her teeth, she ran on, towards the door marked Store Room.

This time, Lloyd waited until they had all caught him up. Then he looked round. 'Ready?'

'Just get on with it!' Ingrid said. Her cheeks were scarlet, and there was sweat running down her nose. 'Open the door!'

'Right. Here we go!' Lloyd pressed down the handle, put his shoulder against the door and pushed — and they found themselves staring straight into the eyes of APE!

Not one, but hundreds and hundreds of them. The room must have been ten metres high and, from floor to ceiling, it was stacked with things printed with that face. Tents and television cabinets. Sweets and sweatshirts. Ring files and rucksacks. From every corner of the room, the ugly, snarling face glared at them, and the slogans yelled in jagged black letters.

DON'T MESS WITH APE!
WANNA MAKE SOMETHING OF IT?
SEE THIS FIST?

In the middle of it all was the snowplough, draped in the books and Babygros and tins of beans through which it had crashed.

It was empty.

'We've lost him!' Ingrid wailed, as they walked into the room. 'He's got away.'

'Indeed I have!' boomed a voice above their heads. 'But *you* won't!'

They looked up. There, in a gallery high up near the roof, was the most terrifying APE! figure of all. The Headmaster. He was holding something small and black and he raised his hand, pointing it towards the door.

175

Dinah's eyes widened in horror. 'It's a remote control! Quick —'

But there was no chance to escape. Before she could even finish speaking, the huge door behind them swung shut, and they heard the click of the automatic lock.

'You have defeated my plans this time,' said the Headmaster, 'but you will never defeat them again. You are trapped. In a moment, I shall press this remote

control again, and the whole Dome will explode. Taking you with it.'

'And you!' Ingrid said, defiantly.

'Oh no. Not me.'

The Headmaster turned slightly, and they saw that he was wearing a large, metal backpack. Lloyd looked bewildered, but Dinah guessed what it was.

'It's a rocket pack, isn't it? You're going to fly out through the roof.'

'Clever to the last, Dinah Hunter,' the Headmaster sneered. 'But your brains won't save you. I shall fly up, out of danger — and *then* I shall press my remote control.'

Harvey went dead white and clutched at Dinah's arm, and she looked round wildly. There *had* to be a way out. It couldn't end like this. But the door was too heavy to move . . .

Then she saw the keys, swinging in the ignition of the snowplough, and she realized that they had one, last chance.

'Lloyd! Could you drive that thing?'

Lloyd frowned. 'Probably. If it's like a car. But I don't see — '

High on the wall, the Headmaster laughed out loud. 'That won't get you out. The door is solid metal, one metre thick.'

'*But I bet the walls aren't,*' Dinah hissed in Lloyd's ear. '*Come on. It's our only chance.*'

He understood at once. With a yelp, he jumped into the snowplough and started up the engine as the others leapt in. Then he put it into gear and pressed his foot down on the accelerator — steering straight for the end wall, below the Headmaster's gallery.

In that glorious second, Dinah knew she was right. Because the Headmaster stopped sneering. He whipped round and pointed his remote control at the roof, pressing it furiously, to open the skylight.

But he was too late. The snowplough crashed into the wall, shattering it into a rain of bricks that clattered on to the roof of the cab. The gigantic figure in the gallery staggered wildly, and then toppled forward, dropping the remote control as he fell.

178

'Keep going!' Dinah yelled, frantically. 'We've got to get out before that remote control hits the floor — '

She didn't need to explain, because they all saw it happen. As the snowplough crashed through to the car-park beyond the Dome, the little black box smashed into the ground, breaking into pieces.

Then, with a great WHOOF, everything behind them exploded. Machines and plants and snow went flying into the air in a shower of shattered panes of glass. And in the middle of the debris was a huge, hairy figure spinning up into the sky. They watched it for as long as they could, but they lost sight of it in the smoke, as the remains of the Dome began to burn.

Uncle Gareth drove them all the way home. He insisted on it. But he seemed confused, and he never said a word when Mrs Hunter asked if the school outing had gone well. He just smiled and accepted a cup of tea.

While Mrs Hunter was making it, Dinah pulled the HP9 cassette out of her pocket.

'Do you mind if —? We ought to watch this, Mum. To find out what happened.'

'These school trips.' Mrs Hunter shook her head and grinned at Uncle Gareth. 'So high-tech.'

He grinned back, vaguely, and Dinah and the others slid off into the sitting-room.

'We don't have to sit through the whole lot,' she said, as she put the cassette into the video. 'But I want to know what happened. Why did all those people decide to march on The Sty? It must be something to do with the subliminal frames.'

'Let's take a look,' Lloyd said.

Dinah fast-forwarded to the first one and pressed the Freeze Frame button. And they all stared.

They were gazing at themselves. Three terrified, open-mouthed children — Ian and Harvey and Mandy — staring up at a fourth, tall, hairy figure.

Ingrid, in the APE! suit.

That was how they had looked in the studio, when Lloyd said, *It's the Headmaster!* The camera had caught them at just that moment, and their faces showed exactly how they felt.

'I hit *both* buttons,' Dinah whispered. 'The one that recorded that frame — *and* the one that substituted it for the marked frames. And so — '

'And so everyone who watched HP9 saw what APE! — what the Headmaster was really like. Just from our faces.' Harvey shuddered again. 'Do we have to go on looking at it?'

'Of course not.' Mandy picked up the remote control and pressed the TV button. The video picture vanished and they found themselves watching the very end of the late News.

'. . . and finally,' the newsreader was saying, 'strange reports are coming in of a giant ape seen *flying* over Wales. There have been several reliable sightings . . .'

A map of Wales flashed up, with six or seven stars dotted over it, to show where the ape had been seen.

180

Then a brown, blurry picture appeared, with the words Amateur Video across the bottom. It was so unsteady, that it was almost impossible to make out what was on the screen.

But Dinah knew. And so did the others.

The newsreader's voice spoke again, sounding amused. 'A helicopter has been sent up, and police confidently expect to apprehend the ape within the next few minutes.'

They did? Dinah wished she could be sure.

Ian shook his head too, staring at the brown, blurry shape as it disappeared into a cloud. 'It would take more than a police helicopter . . .'